ROBYN HOOD: FIGHT FOR FREEDOM

K. M. SHEA

ROBYN HOOD: FIGHT FOR FREEDOM

Copyright © 2022 by K. M. Shea

Cover art by: Wesley Souza

All rights reserved. No part of this book may be used or reproduced in any number whatsoever without written permission of the author, except in the case of quotations embodied in articles and reviews.

This is a work of fiction. Names, characters, places, and incidents are either the product of the author's imagination, or are used fictitiously. Any resemblance to actual persons, living or dead, or historic events is entirely coincidental.

978-1-950635-16-0

www.kmshea.com

❦ Created with Vellum

*For the Champions who have loved Robyn
and the Merry Men and staunchly defended them.*

This book is for you.

PROLOGUE

I turned Crafty around so I could get my last gaze of the camp. The cheerful fires were burning, and it looked dreamy and nostalgic in the starlight. I stared at the camp, burning the image in my mind the way a thirsty man drinks water. I intended for it to be my last look at my Merry Men and our home.

I breathed in, drawing my shoulders back, and directed Crafty into the darkness of Sherwood.

I would no longer be Robin Hood, the Bold and Brave Outlaw of Sherwood Forest.

1

MY NEMESIS IS HONORABLE

The light from the camp quickly disappeared in the trees, and once we were a safe distance away, I urged Crafty into a trot. He tugged on the reins, wanting to go faster, but I was already taking a big chance with riding in the dark, so we kept our pace.

By the time we exited Sherwood Forest, the sun started peeking over the horizon, and I eased Crafty into a canter. It was much smoother than the jarring motion of the trot, which had turned the dull pains in my back into more of a stabbing sensation. The canter soothed my sore muscles, and Crafty gave me a surprisingly pleasant ride.

I slowed him down when we neared Nottingham Castle. Crafty snorted before he walked along, slightly sweaty from his workout. I dismounted and shortened one of my stirrups so it was tucked underneath the flap. I then mounted and sat side saddle, shaking slightly as I supported my leg against Crafty's side. It was an exercise of faith in the horse that I could have gone without experiencing. Riding precariously perched on Crafty's back was not the most comforting of positions.

Thankfully, Nottingham was only a five-minute ride, and I entered the castle without raising suspicion.

Once inside, I wandered for the better part of an hour. I had no idea what I was doing, or even where I should go. I had simply ridden to Nottingham by instinct.

The sun was fully over the horizon when Crafty became irritated. He was hungry, and usually by now I would have let him out to graze in the forest. He tossed his head several times while I dismounted—intending to lead him out of the castle. Instead, the blasted horse dragged me into a nearby stable. I fought him every step of the way, but the giant lug easily pulled me along.

Crafty took a drink from a water trough as I pulled on the reins, which he ignored. While we were fighting, a tall, familiar-looking, blond-haired man entered the stable. He was probably a little older than Little John, although he was built like Much. It took me a few moments before I could place him. He was that steward fellow who followed the Sheriff at the archery contest.

He spotted my horse and smiled. "He's thirsty?"

"Very much so," I dryly said.

"I'm George Comwell, the Sheriff's apprentice," he said with a bow.

My world rocked for a moment. Sheriff's apprentice? This was the man who was apparently behind the greatest schemes to get me?

"Mary Gamwell," I said with a smile to hide my fear. When I realized what I said, I wanted to yelp. Will Scarlet's true last name had rolled off my lips without a thought. "Tell me, Master Comwell. Do many Sheriffs have apprentices?" Maybe there was more than one of them.

George blushed. "Truth be told, it is not my official title. I'm really more of his assistant. I call myself the Sheriff's apprentice because I hope to inherit the position when he is elevated into a new office," he said with a comely grin. "But tell me. Did you say

Gamwell? As in relation to the Earl of Maxfield, William Gamwell?" he asked.

I froze. I was being punished for leaving my men in a cowardly way. That had to be it. What were the chances that I would run into my greatest of foes and that he would know Scarlet's family? "Yes, a distant cousin. Although William did lose his title," I smoothly replied.

"So I heard," George grimly said. "I knew the former Earl of Maxfield. He was a good man."

I nodded, keeping my guard up around this brilliant man. He would *never* suspect me to be Robin Hood because of my gender, but I didn't need him to suspect any kind of connection between me and the outlaws of Sherwood. Even if I was gone there was no sense plaguing my men with worse problems. "I'm not quite sure what happened to him. My mother said he left for Nottingham, but I'm not sure where he went after that," I said.

"You're looking for him then?" George asked.

"Goodness, no," I laughed as I searched my mind for a believable story. "I only met him a handful of times. I came here to see Prince John."

"Ah. Well that's good. You won't find William Gamwell anywhere," George grimly said.

"What do you mean?" I asked as my pulse quickened. Exactly how much did he know about us?

"William Gamwell is no more. He's taken the name of Will Scarlet and he lives in Sherwood Forest. He is one of Robin Hood's men."

"He is?" I said, doing my best to sound astonished instead of terrorized. My fears were confirmed; George was most likely the one dogging down my men and me rather than the fat, brainless Sheriff.

"Yes. No one else knows Will Scarlet's true surname though, I would appreciate it if you kept silent about his business with Robin Hood. It would be better for him if he slipped away before anyone else found out, or if he hangs on the gallows as Will Scarlet while young Gamwell simply disappears," George bitterly said with a confused look on his face, as though he didn't understand why he was telling me all of this.

"You must have greatly admired his father," I said.

"I did. I served as a page under him for several years," George said, pressing his lips together. "Why his *son* chose to dirty the family name and go charging around with the barbaric Robin Hood is beyond me."

I internally shook my fist at him. I am NOT barbaric! "Perhaps he believed in that trite robbing thing Robin Hood is said to be doing. What was it again? Stealing from the rich…"

"To give to the poor," George finished Marian's Outlaw Dream with a weary sigh and a scowl. "I've heard it too many times. The peasants in this shire hold him higher than Prince John—nay, King Richard! He's tearing the government of Nottingham into shambles. If he's as smart as he boasts, he should be able to figure out another way to do this," he said before straightening up. "I'm sorry to place the weight of these matters on you, Lady Mary. Robin Hood has been a temporary curse to the Sheriff, and we are doing our best to catch him," he said with a smile. "In the meantime, is there anything I can do to help you?"

A part of me felt bad. I never thought my enemy would be a good guy. It is easy to rebel against the Sheriff. He's a silly cad. But George…

I glanced at Crafty, who had finally stopped drinking and was eyeing up a hay bale. "Is the feast for Prince John still going on?" I carefully asked.

"Yes," George pleasantly said. "It shall last another week, ending with a masquerade ball."

"Then I'll most certainly need to find a room for myself, as well as a place for my horse to stay," I said, hardly able to believe how daring I was as I motioned to Crafty who had fixed his eerie gaze on George.

George shivered. "That is an intimidating horse you have there," he said as Crafty snarled at him, revealing stained teeth. "Where are your bags?" he asked, peering up and down the barn aisle, as there were none on Crafty.

"A few of my father's men are coming with them later this afternoon. They were held up at the market. I forged my way ahead without them," I sheepishly said as I hung my head. I tried to tell myself over and over that I had nothing to fear from George. After all, I wasn't Robin Hood anymore.

"Excellent," George said with a charming smile. "Let me call a stable hand and he'll take your horse," he said as he walked down the musty aisle. He came back a few minutes later, a scruffy looking boy trotting after him.

"What's 'es name miss?" the stable boy asked as he hesitantly took the reins from my hand.

I paused, thinking for a moment. It would probably be best to give Crafty a fake name as well, just in case.

"Nightmare," I said.

The boy's eyes got bigger as he led Crafty down the stable aisle and into a stall. Crafty wickedly nickered.

George laughed as he gallantly offered his arm, which I took. He led me to the keep, introducing me to lords and ladies as we went. We walked up a seemingly endless tower of stairs before we came to a hallway.

"Here we go," George said, fiddling with a key before he opened it and let me in. It was a medium-sized room with a giant fireplace, several beautiful tapestries on the walls, and a large canopy bed. It was the most expensive place I had ever seen in my young, peasant life.

"Thank you so much, Master Comwell," I gushed. "Are you sure this is… allowable?" I asked.

"Of course," George said with a pleasant smile. "I'm in charge of the rooms. Most lords or ladies would get an audience with the sheriff to get housing, and then he would refer them to me. You've just skipped a few steps. Besides, the Sheriff won't ever remember if he's seen you before or not," he assured me.

Yes... Robin Hood's enemy was, ironically, a charming, honorable man.

George left me after I guaranteed my guards would soon be along. The second he left, I peered out of the door and left my room, locking it behind me with the key he had given me, going to look for my new wardrobe. After all, I am thief.

I wandered around the castle, occasionally sucking in air between my clenched teeth. (My muscles were still plagued by pain). After learning my way around the castle, I moved into action.

First I relieved several pompous lords of their excess change, snagging a nice bag of gold. I then explored the keep and snuck into several ladies' rooms when they were absent. I stole a few dresses, but I mostly took into account what kind of dresses they were wearing.

I took my pilfered goods into my room where I altered—simplifying mostly, it's faster to remove than add on—the dresses with a needle and thread that I had slipped off a palace seamstress. When I was finished, the only thing that could have possibly reminded the previous owners of their dress was the color. (I may be a peasant, but I'm fairly handy with a needle.) The entire time, I did my best to keep my jaw intact and my eyes from popping out of my head. Although I handled many riches, I had seen very little of what they could buy. Everything from the beautiful silk dresses to the polished wood furniture astounded me.

I left the castle in the afternoon and bought a couple of plain, simple dresses from a tailor's shop. I took them back to my room where I added several flourishes and fancy stitching with more stolen thread from the seamstress. I was done by late evening, and I stepped back to admire my work. Although my dresses wouldn't be the most fancy or eye-catching clothes in the castle, they would be simple and appropriate. Besides, I didn't want to catch eyes—I wanted to blend in.

I grinned at my handiwork. The only reason I was able to alter these clothes was because all of my Merry Men were incapable of sewing—except for Robert, an ex-tailor—so I was forced to do most of the camp sewing. It was Robert who had taught me the pretty stitching.

I quickly changed into a lavender colored dress, praising myself for altering the dress so it fit me. I was starved since I hadn't eaten all day and a little irritable as the muscle cramps in my back crept up my spine. I was just about to open my door to leave and eat so I could hurry back to my room and warm my back against the fire, when there was a knock.

I pulled open the door to reveal George.

"Good evening, Lady Mary." He greeted me with a smile.

"Good evening, Master Comwell." I smiled back.

"Oh, just call me George," he said with a grin before he craned his neck. "I see your men have come by." He eyed the many dresses that were thrown across my bed.

"Yes," I said. "But tell me, please, George—are the kitchens still open?" I asked, thinking I would make something for myself.

"Are you joking? The feast hasn't even reached its full height yet!" He grabbed my arm and pulled me down the hallway.

George navigated through twisting passages, several flights of stairs, and numerous doors. We paused when we came to the feasting chamber, a huge room that was merrily lit with roaring fires and torches fastened to the wall. Musicians sat in one corner of the room, playing their chosen instruments, and everyone was roaring and laughing.

Prince John was seated on a gaudy, plush chair at the head of the room, the fat sheriff on his right.

I was thankful George towed me around like a dog on a leash.

I had to work hard to keep from gawking at all of the elegance and riches.

George escorted me to a table of younger, gentle-bred men and woman. "Lady Mary, may I introduce you to Lord Maxine, Lord Edward, and Lady Elizabeth," George said, going down the row. "Gentlemen, and lady, this is Lady Mary Gamwell," George pleasantly said before plopping me into an open seat between the two lords.

A quick calculation said I was in the right spot. The lords and ladies were most likely second or third children of country earls. Marian's schooling kicked in, logically pointing out that they were seated in the back of the room, together, and their clothes were clean and pretty but not impressive. I had seen Marian tear across the countryside on Nearly Dead in more ornamental clothing than what they wore tonight.

I was in the exact position that I wanted to be in, distant yet lordly, but not so royal that I would be expected to act with perfect manners and absolute femininity. If I made a mistake, this trio wouldn't be very likely to notice, much less care.

As I gleefully made these conclusions, I automatically spoke. "Good evening." I smiled, nodding at the lords and lady as George pushed my chair in for me. "It is a pleasure to meet you."

Lady Elizabeth softly smiled and spoke in an equally soft, whispery voice. "Good evening, Lady Mary."

She, unlike Marian, must have been taught to mind her manners.

"Where do you come from, Lady Mary?" Lord Maxine, a dashing man with a playful grin, asked.

I had to mentally shake myself to draw my attention away from the stuffed peacock that was carried past me on a platter and back to my dinner companions.

"Most recently? London," I chattered, my brain quickly filling in the gaps of my story. Making up a disguise on the fly was nerve wracking, but it wasn't like I hadn't done it before. I may have been one of the weakest out of the Merry Men, but I was always the best actor.

"I travel a lot," I said, starting to grow distracted by player who was in the process of swallowing fire. (*Fire!*)

"Really?" Lord Edward asked, his left eyebrow popping up in surprise. "Your parents allow you to?"

Clearly I had made a mistake.

I took my mind off the fire eater and thought back to Marian's stories, weaving together a reasonable explanation for traveling. "Well, it's not like I see a lot of new places," I reasoned. "I'm constantly passed between four manors. One belongs to my mother's relations, one my father's, one manor is a brother's, and the last castle I stay at is that of a dear friend's," I supplied.

"Oh, I see," Lord Edward said, accepting my lies. Nobility did leave often to go visit each other. Marian's trip to Queen Eleanor's court was a perfect example of that.

"Are you the one who owns that devil of a horse that arrived this morning?" Lord Maxine asked with another grin.

"Yes," I calmly replied, taking a sip of my wine (I was drinking *wine*!) after nibbling at the positively delicious roasted boar. "Has news of him spread so far already?"

"He is quite infamous, but no. I only heard of him because he took a chunk out of my Winther's hide," Lord Maxine said.

"I've seen this horse he refers to. Coal black and rather…" Lord Edward searched for an appropriate adjective that would properly describe Crafty without offending me.

"Crafty?" I suggested. "His name is Nightmare."

"Aptly named," Lord Maxine said under his breath.

"He sounds like he would be too much for a female to handle," Lady Elizabeth dubiously said.

"It's not so much that he's difficult to control, he is just exceedingly foul tempered. He happens to hate me less than he hates everyone else. We get along quite nicely," I soothed the gentle lady.

"He has a nice look to him. Excellent confirmation," Lord Edward said.

I didn't have a hope of understanding what he was talking about. "Um, thank you?"

"I suppose you wouldn't know his sire or dame?" Lord Maxine piped in.

"Lord Maxine," Lady Elizabeth said in her whispery voice, sounding quite scandalized. "That is not decent dinner talk, much less the way to talk to a lady."

"It's fine, Eliza," Lord Maxine said. "We're cousins," he explained for my benefit.

I glanced back and forth between my dinner companions. Edward did not seem terribly bothered by Maxine's interrogation of my horse, even if Elizabeth was. Maxine seemed too informal to be a proper judge, so I resolved to use Edward as my scale of normalcy.

"He was given to me by a friend," I carefully said. "I do not know his pedigree."

"Now that's a shame," Lord Maxine complained.

"Lady Elizabeth, where are you from?" I asked. The easiest way to get away with my masquerade was to engage a different person, drawing the attention off me.

It worked well; Lady Elizabeth softly chatted through the rest of the meal.

I was stuck there for a full hour. Saying stuck sounds negative, but by the end of that hour, I was ready to start crying in pain. My back muscles were cramping again. The hum of the music and the steady throb of loud voices in the hall crawled into my skull and created the headache of the century. My eyes hurt from staring at everything, and a pin I had slipped in my dress to keep the waist tight had wriggled loose and was stabbing me in the gut. I hurt so much I decided I would leave, never mind if the feast was over yet or not. I actually almost fell to the floor when I tried to stand. I managed to steady myself with some help from Lord Maxine, who automatically reached out and grabbed me.

"Lady Mary, are you feeling well?" he asked, his voice laced with concern as he stood as well.

"I am a little tired. I believe it may be best if I turn in for the night." I did my best to smile in spite of the pain that wracked my body. I was still getting over my sickness, but at least now I was hurting less than I had in previous days.

"Lady Mary, do you need anything?" George asked, materializing in front of my table.

"I'm fine, George, thank you," I smiled, finding it amusing that he, the Sheriff's apprentice, would be worried about my wellbeing. "I am perhaps more weary than I would like to admit. I believe I shall retire to my room."

"I'll escort her ladyship back to her room, Master George, don't worry," Maxine grinned dashingly.

"I'm quite capable of reaching my quarters on my own," I insisted.

"Thank you, Lord Maxine. She is housed in the same hall as Lady Elizabeth," George said, bowing at the young lord before returning to other guests, chatting with them with a pleasant smile.

"This way, Lady Mary," Maxine directed, steering us out of the great hall. I stopped to wave farewell to Edward and Elizabeth.

The musicians plucked and piped on their instruments, and dancing had started. The feast would probably go on hours longer. Hours that I would thankfully not be present for.

I surprised myself by quite easily remembering the way back to my room.

"Are you sure you'll be tolerable alone, Lady Mary? Do you not have a ladies maid who could assist you?" Maxine asked.

"If I need help, I'll call for one. Thank you, Lord Maxine." I smiled between clenched teeth before I backed into my room, shutting the door in Maxine's fine face.

I immediately barred the door and started ripping off my dress. I changed into a nightgown and huddled in front of the fire, warming my stiff back against the flames. "Should have brought some hose and a tunic or two with me," I grumbled.

The fire cracked, but besides that my room was quiet. I yawned. "This must be the first time I've been alone since Will Stutely christened Little John," I laughed. "It's quiet," I observed after several moments. "Very quiet."

That night, I slept for the first time on a mattress stuffed with feathers. While it was delightfully soft, I had a hard time falling asleep. There were no hooting owls or panting dogs. Crafty did not wickedly snicker in his pen, and Much's snores weren't audible. I couldn't hear my men shift on their guard duty or laugh as they shared a story around the fire.

I missed them.

"It's a pity," I whispered to my silent room. "I don't think they're missing me."

2

MARIAN AT NOTTINGHAM

I spent three relatively carefree days in the castle before I began to realize that I could only bum off Nottingham Castle for so long. In those three days, I slowly finished recuperating from my sickness. I was my own jailer, and often slept for hours on end to provide an excuse so I wouldn't have to attend those wretched banquets. (The food was good, and they were quite entertaining… but after the third night of feasting, I was beginning to see why Marian complained of them so.)

"I believe I am almost healed." I did a handstand, testing out my back. It barely protested. "This is good. I'll have to move on soon." I tumbled out of my handstand and waded through the mess of my dresses. "Tis a shame, but I'll have to leave most of my wardrobe behind. Crafty can't carry them all, and if I'm traveling on the road, it would be wiser to go disguised as a male."

I walked over to my dressing table, which was now cluttered with hair pins and veils. (I lifted them out of several different rooms over the previous days.)

There was a soft tap on the door—Lady Elizabeth probably. Ever since George stuck me with the trio on that first feast, they were my daily companions. I swore underneath my breath. I was dressed in nothing but a nightshirt.

"Yes?" I called through the door.

"Lady Mary, it's me, Elizabeth," Elizabeth timidly said through the door. "I was about to go down to the castle gardens. Would you care to join me?"

I silently groaned and kicked a dress. "Of course. I'll be ready in ten minutes."

"Thank you, I'll return to my room until you're ready," Elizabeth softly replied before her light steps signaled she had walked away.

It wasn't that I minded Lady Elizabeth; I just *really* didn't feel like squeezing myself into another one of my blasted dresses. Even worse, going out would mean I had to style my hair.

I hastily threw on a new dress, one that was dark blue with little bits of white lace. Feeling entirely irritated with the idea of pinning up my hair, I daringly twined my hair into a braid, which is what I often did before my Robin Hood days when I had long hair. Unfortunately, my hair was not as long now. To keep from looking stupid with a braid that ended with three hairs, I tucked the back half of my hair into netting and pinned it to my skull.

I emerged from my room in a wild whirlwind exactly ten minutes later, ready for my walk with Lady Elizabeth. I silently padded down the hallway (old habits of moving quietly die slowly) and knocked on Elizabeth's door.

Elizabeth opened her door and stepped out as one of her dressing maids finished tying a ribbon in her hair. "Good morn, Lady Mary."

"Good morning, Lady Elizabeth."

"I invited Lords Edward and Maxine as well. I believe they're already in the gardens," she said, taking my arm in a girlish gesture of friendship.

"Sounds like a regular party," I joked as we skipped down the hallway. Well, I skipped, but Elizabeth had to scurry to keep pace.

We toppled down the stairs, and Elizabeth got us lost only once before we stumbled into the beautiful gardens, which were just outside the castle keep. (Elizabeth did not navigate around the castle as easily as I did. Of course, Elizabeth was not an outlaw who depended upon sneaking around and pick-pocketing royals to keep up her front.)

"Lady Elizabeth, Lady Mary, you look especially gorgeous this bright morning," Lord Maxine shouted with an enthusiasm and volume that even *I* knew was uncivil.

Lord Edward breathed in only slightly sharper than usual. "Good morning, Lady Elizabeth, Lady Mary," he said in his gravelly voice.

"Good morning Lord Edward," Elizabeth curtsied, ignoring her cousin.

"Good morning," I chorused.

"It is such delightful weather we're having today, is it not, Lord Edward?" Elizabeth asked Edward, her eyes fastened on him. Even I, a barbarian according to George, knew Elizabeth was smitten with Edward.

"It is stupendous weather. I fear it shall grow overly warm in the afternoon," Edward returned. Whenever the two E's chatted, they were always dreadfully boring.

Judging by the way Maxine was rolling his eyes behind his friends' backs, he agreed with me.

Edward and Elizabeth turned and started walking up a path, Elizabeth still dragging me along by the arm.

"It does grow dreadfully hot in the summer, and it makes me so fatigued," Elizabeth commented, not noticing when Maxine yanked me out of her grasp and held me back a few steps.

"Hang back and let them walk farther ahead. Eliza won't mind; she might even be grateful. Besides, those two are about as interesting as watching candle wax harden," Maxine scoffed as we were led into a maze of shrubberies.

I couldn't hold back the quirk of a grin that spread across my lips for a split second. Maxine caught the glimpse of my humor and smiled back at me.

"So Lady Mary, how is your dear, devil horse?" he asked.

"Nightmare? He is as happy as his disposition allows him to be."

"I should think so. They can't keep horses in the stalls next to him or he rips a chunk out of their hide," Maxine laughed.

I frowned. "He got out of the stables again yesterday. I caught him when he was just about to push his way into the kitchens. Next time I wish they would let me know he's being bad," I complained as we made a sharp turn around a shrub-wall.

"Oh, come now. It's hardly befitting for a lady to be running around after her horse. At least, you better not let Eliza hear of you doing that anyway," Maxine chuckled as we continued to meander after Edward and Elizabeth.

"So how is your horse, Winther?" I asked.

"He is fine. Would you care to accompany me on a ride this fair afternoon, Lady Mary?" Maxine asked. "I'm sure Eliza and Lord Edward would join us as well."

"Where do you plan to ride?" I asked, hoping he wouldn't be an idiot and decide to venture into—.

"I was thinking of going to Sherwood Forest," Maxine admitted.

Idiot. Idiot. Idiot.

"I believe that would be a rather foolish plan, Lord Maxine," I said. I couldn't help that the usual tone of mirth and gentleness that I tried to keep in my voice for the role of "Lady Mary" drained out as I became serious.

"A band of thieves lives there. It's not a good place for nobility to tread through."

"So you've heard of him as well. Robin Hood, I mean," Maxine said as we rounded a corner of shrubs, still a few feet behind the E's.

"Of course. Who has—" my eyes widened before I swung

back around the corner and flattened myself against the shrubbery wall. Elizabeth and Edward had led us out of the green maze and into an open courtyard that was filled with beautiful flowers.

And in that open courtyard, with hair so blonde and eyes so blue, was my best friend Marian, who had by now doubtlessly heard of the disappearing act I had pulled.

Marian was the last person I wanted to see. Not only could she blow my cover, but she could, and would, drag me back to Sherwood Forest kicking and screaming. Or worse yet: she would tell the Merry Men where to find me.

I dearly loved Marian, but I knew I couldn't count on her in this instance. It was best to keep out of sight and leave the castle premises as soon as possible. If Marian was here, it was likely she would be at the feast tonight, and possibly every night until the masquerade ball.

I muttered several curses under my breath as Maxine curiously stepped back to observe me with a cocked eyebrow.

I ignored him and kept swearing. "Just my bloody luck," I groaned. I would have to leave as soon as possible; the second I could wrench myself away from the E's and Maxine. The moment I got back to my room, I would split. Marian couldn't find me. I couldn't be dragged back to Sherwood. I wouldn't!

"Are you well, Lady Mary?" he asked.

"Absolutely," I said as I peeked back around the bush.

Marian was still there.

She had a smile pasted on her face, one of those fake ones she perfected so she could lie straight-faced to her mother when she asked Marian if she had completed her sewing exercise of the day. Marian was nodding her head in an engaged manner as she spoke softly with her companion, a dark haired, knightly looking man I vaguely recognized.

"She must hate his guts," I muttered. "She only looks like that when she's praying for someone's painful death."

Maxine also peered around the bushes. "Oh, do you know Lady Marian?"

I snapped out of it. "Who?" I prettily asked.

"Lady Marian, Robin Hood's supposed maiden. Oh goodness."

"What? What?" I asked, about ready to shake Maxine.

"That's Sir Guy of Gisborne she's with," Maxine observed.

"Who?" I asked.

"Sir Guy of Gisborne," Maxine repeated.

"What nutty parent would force that curse of a name on their child," I muttered under my breath as I watched Edward and Elizabeth continue through the courtyard without us.

"His, obviously," Maxine supplied.

I rolled my eyes and flipped back against the shrubbery, pressing my head against the leaves and branches. "I can't stay here, not anymore," I muttered.

"So are we just going to sit here at the corner, or shall we backtrack?" Maxine offered.

"Pardon?"

"You are obviously against going into the courtyard. Come, we can go back the way we came. I'll tell Eliza I got us lost. She'll believe it," Maxine said, strolling back up the path we had come down. "Are you coming?"

I hurried after Maxine, mentally packing as we went.

I WASN'T able to elegantly back away from Lord Maxine until mid-afternoon. I stewed and waited in my room, surfacing only to tell Lady Elizabeth to proceed to the feasting hall without me. I had stowed the two dresses I wanted to take in a saddle pack, and pilfered a tunic that belonged to one of the castle servants. I would hide the dresses and leave at dusk, just when the feast would start to grow in size.

Eventually the time came. I wrapped the remaining dresses

and left them behind in my room. Still wearing my dark blue dress from the afternoon, I shouldered my saddle packs and made my way through the castle.

Nobody gave me a second glance as I confidently hustled down the stairs. The scuffling servants didn't bat an eyelash as I swished past them in my full skirts. Within minutes, I had successfully navigated my way out to the stables.

When I entered the stable, Crafty, alone in his back corner stall, stuck his head out and narrowed his eyes when they landed on me.

"We're going, Crafty," I told him, slinging the saddle bags over his stall door. I tapped my fingers on the door and considered the dim stables. "I need to find your tack first."

I dug around in the stable for a while until I found Crafty's saddle and bridle. They were neatly placed on a saddle rack and bridle hook, the last place I happened to glance at.

I had brushed Crafty earlier in the morning, so I only needed to throw on a blanket and the saddle before sliding Crafty's bridle on.

I tossed the saddle bags across Crafty's back before I began to lead him out of the stable.

I got him to the courtyard but just when I was about to swing upon his back into a most unlady-like astride position, I was interrupted.

"It's a little late to be riding, Lady Mary."

It was Maxine.

"Why the sudden departure, Lady Mary? Are the feasts really *that* unbearable?"

It was worse than I thought. He brought George with him. George, my puppy dog enemy whom I had foolishly began to think of as a friend.

I grumbled through my teeth before spinning on my heels and facing the duo, flashing my most charming smile. "Of course not, Master George, Lord Maxine."

"Does it have something to do with Lady Marian then?" Maxine asked.

I had to keep myself from gaping at him.

"Lord Maxine mentioned after seeing the lady you acted... *strangely*. Do you not get along with her? Don't feel like you have to flee her presence. *Lots* of ladies choose not to associate with Lady Marian," George gallantly said.

"She's cracked," Maxine bluntly said before George sharply elbowed him. "I mean, she is difficult to get along with."

I wondered if I could throw myself on Crafty and disappear into the night before they cried an alarm.

"The point is, Lady Mary, I hope you don't feel like you have to leave because Lady Marian has come," George calmly explained. "I had hoped you were enjoying your time as a guest of Nottingham Castle."

"Stay a little longer, Mary," Maxine encouraged. "I can shield you from Maid Marian. We just have to start talking about Robin Hood whenever she's in earshot and that mother of hers will drag her off."

"You are both mistaken," I nervously laughed. "Lady Marian has nothing to do with my departure."

"Then why are you leaving?" Maxine, ever un-gentlemanly, had the nerve to ask.

Silence fell on our group as I tried to come up with a reasonable explanation and realized that there *wasn't* one because Marian really *was* the reason, although not in the capacity that Maxine and George thought.

"Thought so," Maxine said in a tiny voice so George wouldn't elbow him again.

"Please reconsider your sudden departure, Lady Mary," George handsomely pleaded, walking up to me. He made a movement as though to pet Crafty before he remembered my horse's temperament.

I considered my options. I could say yes and try to sneak out again in the days to come… but it wasn't like I had a plan anyway. My brain was currently occupied with the sole thought of fleeing Nottingham. What would I do when I left the castle? I had my male clothes to change into, but I had no plan beyond that.

"At least stay for the masquerade party in two nights," George reasoned. He was genuinely upset that I seemed to be so set on leaving.

I sighed and gave in. "Alright." I didn't really have a choice. Besides, as long as I was careful, I could surely avoid Marian, especially if Maxine was under the impression that I wanted to avoid her as much as possible. "I shall stay until your masquerade party, George."

George's face split into a grin. "I am very glad to hear that, Lady Mary."

"We'll have such fun," Maxine insisted, coming up on my other side. "And don't worry about Lady Marian. We shan't have any problems avoiding *her*. Sir Guy has been practically glued to her side since her arrival."

Together George and Maxine herded me back to the stable, assisting me in untacking Crafty. (Maxine chattered at me, saying it was very daring to be leaving in the middle of the night without my dresses and men. Apparently he presumed I had left my clothing behind for my imaginary guards to handle.)

Some minutes later, George and I strolled toward the castle, Maxine roaming in front of us, my saddle packs slung over his shoulder.

"I am very glad to hear you were so eager to leave only because of Lady Marian's arrival," George announced.

I curiously glanced sideways at him. "Why else would I leave?"

George looked rather uncomfortable. "I thought you might have heard some of the rumors."

I cocked an eyebrow. "Rumors?"

George looked rather cross with himself. "Being a deputy to

the Sheriff I hear all the news regarding Robin Hood, and, well, apparently his band of outlaws are in an upheaval."

"Why?" I asked, like any good, nosy lady would.

"Supposedly...Robin Hood has disappeared."

Around this time, I began to wonder if a few of my men were leaking information to the Sheriff. How could George know this? He answered my question himself, actually.

"They're getting desperate—his men, that is. Will Scarlet, I mean your cousin, William Gamwell, appeared in the Nottingham's market today, shouting for Robin Hood at the top of his lungs, unabashedly appearing as one of Robin's Merry Men. Reports from neighboring villages say that Little John was doing the same in village squares. About three Merry Men accompanied them each time."

I almost hissed. The dynamic duo of stupidity was going to get caught, or worse, hung!

"In both cases, they were able to successfully slip away," George said, sounding disgruntled. "But next time, I assure you, they will not."

In my mind, I so passionately prayed they would that I didn't notice some odd feet behind us, another couple had taken to following George, Maxine, and I.

It was Marian and that wretched Sir Guy.

And as they trailed after us, Marian studied me in my lady disguise with intense blue eyes. "Robyn?" she quietly whispered to herself.

I unknowingly walked in front of her, listening to George's vows to capture me.

LORD MAXINE WAS true to his word. Each day Maxine, complete with Lord Edward and Lady Elizabeth, would drag me down to the lower part of Nottingham Castle (the markets, the shops, the stalls) during the morning, and would then drag me out for rides in the afternoon.

Marian famously did not rise until noon, and after that, her mother usually forcibly paraded her around the castle grounds, usually with a knight or two, like Sir Guy, trailing in their wake like dogs, so I didn't see Marian once until the night of the masquerade ball.

Truth be told, I believe Lord Edward enjoyed our excursions to the markets in the morning. He was far more eager and attentive when examining livestock or haggling with a weapons dealer than he was when stuffed in the gardens, chatting about the weather. Lady Elizabeth fared as well as she could. She didn't like it, but she bore it for Edward's sake.

The masquerade ball had Elizabeth in a tizzy. She spent the morning getting ready for it, even though Maxine, Edward, and I visited the lower city, as was custom for our group.

While in the city I, on the sly, managed to buy a lovely, burgundy mask with little roses sewn into the corners. My dress was the same shade of burgundy and was one of my few ensembles that I truly enjoyed. The sleeves were long and open with little roses sewn into the cuffs. It was a V-neck and had pretty veiling over the red skirts.

Lord Maxine was to be my escort for the night. I suspected that George might have bullied him into it, but Maxine was willing enough.

I left my room that evening, meeting Lord Maxine at the stairwell. He admired my costume and mask most beautifully. "You look positively stunning Lady Mary. Or should I refer to you as Lady Rose?" He winked.

Maxine was dressed as a crusader. He wore a white linen tunic with the red cross and the silvery boots and chain mail gloves.

"Thank you, Lord Maxine," I said, a smile briefly gracing my lips as I fussed with a strand of hair. (I had taken the trouble to pin my hair up tonight.)

Although a large part of me, the peasant part, was excited about the prospect of attending, I was worried. I would be able to leave Nottingham Castle tomorrow, but I didn't have a clue what I should do when I left.

Maxine took my quiet silence in stride and chivalrously led me to the feasting hall, where Lady Elizabeth and Lord Edward were waiting for us. Lady Elizabeth looked positively exquisite dressed in a beautiful white gown that completed her swan disguise. Lord Edward was dressed like a knight from a chess board.

Lady Elizabeth and I gushed over each other's dresses, but I fell silent when Marian entered the room, on the arm of Sir Guy of Gisborne.

Marian was wearing a dress that was colored with the muted tones of the forest. She wore soft leather shoes and kid suede gloves that looked suspiciously liked mine. Slung across her back was a rabbit skin quiver, and perched on her head was a brown hat, complete with a pheasant feather.

Marian was dressed as Robin Hood.

Marian was dressed as me.

3

MY UNDOING

The crowds murmured and shifted, staring at the lively lass who dared to dress like an outlaw in front of Prince John.

The Prince nervously laughed when he saw her. His nervous giggle was more of a whining noise, much like the sound Much makes when Will Stutely sits on his head. Marian smiled prettily, looking as unassuming and innocent as possible.

The awkward moment blew over without a problem. It was almost just as well Marian had daringly dressed up as Robin Hood because no one saw the tall, gallant gentlemen who entered the room after her.

Elizabeth turned away from Marian, eager to lay claim on Edward's attention. "Shall we dance?" she suggested, gesturing to the dance floor where couples were already spinning.

Edward wordlessly offered his palm. Elizabeth glowed and took it before the two swept off to the dance floor.

I sourly watched them leave. Dancing was one of the few things I would never be able to fake. Dancing around the May Pole is one thing. Dancing with nobility is an entirely different matter.

"Do you want to dance?" Maxine asked me with obvious hesitation and dislike. Apparently, I was not alone in my distaste.

"No," I emphatically replied.

Maxine looked utterly relieved. "Great," he brightly said before correcting himself. "I mean, w-what a shame," he sheepishly laughed.

By now I was comfortable enough with Maxine that I would occasionally let my peasant-y-ness get the better of me. My next action was a perfect example.

"A man eating fire!" I shouted before hurrying off to stare at one of the players.

Maxine followed and watched me with great amusement as I gazed wide-eyed at the players who were hired for tonight's entertainment. The man had already swallowed the fire, and breathed it out the way a dragon would. He then proceeded to juggle torches, never burning himself on the brilliant flames.

My eyes were practically popping out of my mask ten minutes later when Maxine pulled me away, handing me a goblet of wine.

"They were just about to bring out the trained bear," I muttered, disappointed.

Maxine laughed, a loud, fun sound. "I will never tire of your company, Lady Mary," he roared.

I couldn't help but grin in return before I cast my eyes over the crowd and had a heart attack.

Two men were walking together, carefully searching the room. One was a mountain of a man, a *giant* who looked as strong as an ox. The other was tall and limber and carried a sword with the assurance of a man who knew how to use it. They could only be Little John and Will Scarlet.

I wildly twisted around, trying to avoid their stares. Marian must have seen me and tattled after all. The snitch.

"Lady Mary, are you well?" Maxine inquired.

"Yes, I'm perfectly fine," I said as I slowly side stepped until I was hiding behind Maxine's body. "I just saw some acquaintances I would rather not run into at this moment," I said as I looked for the nearest exit.

There was no way around it, I would have to leave. *Now.*

To my surprise, Maxine grabbed my hands and swung me out to the dance floor.

"Wh-what are you doing?" I hissed as Maxine twirled me around.

"It's those two strapping young men who entered after Lady Marian, right? They'll be less likely to spot you in this whirling mob," Maxine logically pointed out.

"Thank you, however did you know?" I asked, bumbling on my feet like a hobbled horse.

"Your facial reaction was pretty obvious when you spotted them," Maxine dryly said, spinning me in a wild circle.

"Perhaps," I agreed.

Maxine snorted. "You are much more mysterious, Lady Mary, than I originally thought."

"What makes you say that?" I asked, nearly ramming into a beautiful girl who was dressed to resemble a fox.

"Because with each passing day, you seem to run into more and more acquaintances you would like to avoid," Maxine said, spinning me into his arms. "Are you an angry woman, Mary?"

"Excuse me?" I sputtered before he swung me away from him again.

"Do you make enemies easily?"

"I never said Marian was my enemy," I countered, narrowly avoiding a man dressed like a court jester.

Maxine arched an eyebrow while reaching out to grab my waist with his free arm. "You don't say?" he asked.

"Excuse me," rumbled a deep voice I would never be able to misplace. "Could I have this dance?"

I slowly dragged my panicked eyes away from Maxine and settled them on Little John, who was clogging up the flow of the dance while he patiently waited for my response, his hand outstretched.

Maxine opened his mouth to deny Little John's request while he tugged me backwards, but I moved first.

"Thank you, Lord Maxine, for the lovely dance. I shall return to you shortly," I said, pulling my hand out of his grip before transferring it over to Little John's.

"Are you sure, Lady Mary?" Maxine asked, eyeing Little John.

"Yes. It's no use, I've been caught," I said with a half-hearted smile before I allowed Little John to pull me away.

Little John led me through the dance floor, stopping when we were next to an open balcony door that was on the outer perimeter of the room. We could talk in relative privacy while pretending to dance without bothering the other dancers.

"Lady Mary, is it?" Little John asked.

"Yes," I crisply replied. "And what is your name, sir?" I asked with false cheer.

"You know my name, Robyn," Little John hissed.

"You seem to have mistaken me for someone else, kind sir," I said, my voice turning cold.

Little John snapped his head back, as though I had physically slapped him. "Robyn, I-I'm sorry," he stammered.

"For what?" I spat. "For running an unfair contest? For demanding to take my place? For driving me out of Sherwood?"

"I didn't mean—I'm sorry," Little John pleaded.

"Of course you are," I agreed. "I hope you'll be very happy as the new leader of the Merry Men. Good luck, you'll need it."

"What?" Little John startled. "Robyn, you have to come back with us!"

"I don't have to do *anything*," I harshly laughed.

Little John stared at me from behind his mask, dismay oozing past the black edges.

"Here, allow me," said a second unmistakable voice.

Will Scarlet didn't give Little John an option. He swept in, cutting in between the two of us. He took my hand and elegantly twirled me in a swinging motion that was far more careful than Lord Maxine's.

"Robyn," Will greeted as Little John backed off.

"Scarlet," I replied.

"I must admit, you outdid yourself. Marian told me she had a hard time believing it was you. Really, the courts of *Prince John* were the last place I would have expected you to go to. Very cunning," Will Scarlet praised, circling around me for the dance.

"Oh, I learned from the best," I said with a clear smile.

Will Scarlet did not cringe or stumble as Little John had. "That may be so," he agreed. "Crafty is aptly named, after all."

I rolled my eyes.

"Now that all the little parties and feasts are done, you'll come back," he stated more than asked.

I snorted. "Not in your lifetime, Will Scarlet," I said, stepping to the side to continue our awkward dance.

"You're our leader, Robyn. You know we'll never survive without you," Will said, his blue eyes practically stabbing me.

"You previously made it very clear, Scarlet, that my leadership was no longer necessary. Little John will be an excellent replacement, I assure you."

"You're wrong, Robyn. We need you. Our camp has fallen into shambles. The Merry Men went wild when we discovered you left. Nearly half of the company wanted to storm Nottingham to search for you. It was all Little John and I could do to keep them calm. Of course, Much and Will Stutely wouldn't help us; they won't help anyone but you."

"I see, so I am a necessary crank in the mechanics of the Merry Men? How thoughtful of you to invite me to return to such warmth. I'm sorry, but I'm going to have to refuse," I scoffed.

"That's not it, Robyn. Why can't you see that we lov—" Will Scarlet started before I cut him off.

"You are sorely mistaken, Scarlet, if you think you can butter me up into returning. As far as I'm concerned, you made your voice on who should be the new leader *quite* clear. Good luck, Will Scarlet. I hope you can free the King," I said before disengaging my hand from his and walking away.

I headed for Maxine, vaguely registering that George was shouting in the Sheriff's ear as I stalked away from Scarlet.

"Robyn, wait," Will Scarlet hissed, grabbing my wrist.

Just as he wrenched me around, the Sheriff shouted. "Guards, seize those two! They are outlaws of England!"

"Seize them!" Prince John echoed, gripping his skinny little neck with jewel covered fingers.

For one wild second, I thought he meant me. My heart stopped, and I froze. It was only when the guards quickly surrounded Little John, who was two feet behind Will Scarlet, that I realized I was being overlooked.

"It's Little John and Will Scarlet!" a soldier shouted, stepping forward to rip the identical, black masks off my men's faces.

Several women shrieked, Marian cursed like a sailor, and the music halted with an abrupt screech. The dancers fled the dance floor, watching the soldiers with wide eyes.

Will Scarlet looked wild. His blue eyes swam with panic and he shifted his weight, as though to leap in front of me and shield me. He still held my wrist in his hand.

"Step away from the lady, sir," George gravely ordered, pushing his way through the crowd until he popped out near us.

Will Scarlet did not move a muscle, but transferred his gaze to George.

George carefully walked past the guards and hissed at Will. "I know Lady Gamwell is your cousin, Scarlet. If you have any remaining care for her or your family name, you will give in without a fuss."

Will Scarlet slowly slid his searing blue eyes back to my face. He stared at me for a second before a smile cracked across his face. He leaned in until his lips touched my ear and whispered.

"They need you, Robyn. I don't regret coming here, not if it means you'll return to Sherwood. You're our hope, Robyn. We need you. We love you," he uttered before pulling back, his cheek grazing mine. I blushed a brilliant red hue when he gently kissed the corner of my mouth before stepping back.

"Lead the way, wishful sheriff," Will Scarlet laughed in a careless manner, flicking his hand through the air while a soldier removed Will's sword from his side.

George twisted and stalked off, Will Scarlet trailing behind him with an armed escort. One soldier held a silver sword pressed to Will's back, pricking him between his shoulder blades. Little John followed, his arms held behind his back by two soldiers, but he gave a long, studious look as he passed by. His eyes flicked back and forth between Scarlet and me before he was hauled out of the room.

My heart stopped in my chest as I watched my two best men, my Little John, my Scarlet, walk out of the room, most likely to the dungeons, and certainly to their death.

I took two steps forward and opened my mouth, as though to cry out. Marian caught me by the wrist.

I spun around to face her, looking stricken. She shook her head. "You can't. You'll destroy everything they've worked for. They're sacrificing themselves, *Lady Mary*, for your sake," Marian said.

I ripped my arm out of her grip and backed up, my mind reeling.

The crowd whispered and gossiped, a variable storm of lowered voices as Little John and Will Scarlet were paraded out of the room.

Maxine, Elizabeth, and Edward materialized at my side.

"Lady Mary, are you alright?" Edward asked in a concerned voice.

"We saw what happened. How *horrible*," Elizabeth whispered in a soothing voice.

"Would you like me to escort you back to your room?" Maxine quietly asked, gently grasping one of my elbows.

Marian faded into the mass of people that flooded the dance floor.

"Lady Mary?"

"Mary."

"I'm fine," I blurted, backing away from my friends. "I'm fine," I repeated. "I just need to go—" I managed to choke out before pushing my way through the crowd, hurrying through the hall.

"Lady Mary!"

"Mary, wait!"

I ignored my friends' calls and skidded into the main hallway. I rushed down the hallway, taking several sharp turns before I skid onto an open balcony. I was only one floor above the ground level.

I didn't check for observers, I just hiked up my skirts and jumped the railing. I landed with a dull thunk and straightened up before hurrying through the small courtyard, mentally adjusting my priorities. I would get Crafty and head to Sherwood Forest. I could muster up a small group of men and be back by dawn to infiltrate Nottingham. I couldn't leave Little John and Will Scarlet to die. I couldn't.

The air started to resonate with the sound of dozens of ringing church bells. Soldiers shouted across walkways, and the castle jumped to life.

I was almost to the stable when a great force knocked me off my feet, tackling me to the ground.

"Got… you…," Marian huffed, rolling off my back as she wheezed.

"Marian?" I groaned, blinking to clear the stars from my vision.

"Evening," she greeted.

"What did you do that for?" I moaned, wincing as I pushed myself off the ground.

"You… wouldn't…. stop," she heaved, still catching her breath. "Too… fast."

"Of course," I irritably snapped. "I have to get moving. I need to act quickly and get to Sherwood For—"

"It's no good," Marian interrupted, finally regaining her wind.

"What?"

"It's no good. Didn't you hear the bells? The Sheriff has ordered for all Nottingham to lock up. All of the gates are up, there's no way in or out. He's trapping us like rats. We're on our own for this round," Marian said. "The castle won't open until after Little John and Will Scarlet hang tomorrow morning."

"How do you know?" I asked with numb lips.

"If you had stayed an extra five moments, you would have heard him announce it," Marian snorted as she stood up. Her green dress was smeared with grime. "You really shouldn't go dashing around like that, you know. Not only does it make you look suspicious, it's incredibly hard to try and catch up to you."

I pushed myself into a standing position, ignoring my spoiled dress. "I have to save them, Marian. I can't let them die," I said, my voice breaking.

"Don't get your petticoats in a knot. I never said we wouldn't save them," Marian clucked. "But we need a plan, and I just happen to have one," Marian grinned, sliding her rabbit skin quiver off her shoulders. She removed the three arrows, turned the quiver upside down, and violently shook it. Clothes fell out of the quiver. Lincoln green clothes.

"What did you have in mind?" I asked, fingering the material.

Marian wolfishly smiled. "You're going to love it," she promised.

I didn't, for the record.

THE FOLLOWING MORNING, when the sun barely rose over the horizon, I stood outside the castle keep with a fretting Lady Elizabeth, a grave Lord Maxine, and a quiet Lord Edward.

"Are you sure you won't stay any longer?" Maxine asked, pinning me with his sad, brown cow eyes.

"I can't," I said, fussing with the hunter green velvet material of my dress. "With Will hanging today, there will soon be a scandal, and I can't bear the thought of watching it. I must go comfort my aunt," I said. Under Marian's direction, I was playing the "mourning relative" card because of my supposed connection to Will Scarlet.

"I wish you would stay. I'll miss you," Elizabeth said before hugging me on an impulse. I was touched; she clearly was regretting that I really was leaving her.

"I wish you well. But Lady Mary… if any were to think badly of you because of this… situation, they would truly be fools," Edward sincerely said.

I smiled, surprised that the trio had become my friends over such a short amount of time. "Thank you. Thank you ever so much," I said. "But I really feel that I should leave," I said, backing towards Marian's giant carriage behind me.

George Comwell exited the stables in a quick walk.

"I'm glad I caught you," he said, approaching the carriage with a sad smile. He stopped a short distance away from me and said in a quiet voice "I am sorry about this, Mary. But he has broken the law. It's necessary."

I nodded. "I understand," I said, even though in my heart I wanted to bash George's face in.

George tried to give me a smile before he offered me his hand. I took it, and we strolled over to Marian's carriage. "I've already sent word of your arrival to the main gate. After a quick search, they'll let you out."

"Thank you, George. I can never repay you," I said, knowing that George was pulling strings to grant me an exit.

"It's the least I could do," George said, handing me up into the carriage.

"So you've mended the fence with Lady Marian, I take it?" Maxine asked, squinting up at me as I entered the carriage, carefully sat down on the plush red seats, and stuck my head out of a window.

"Yes, how did you know?" I smiled.

"Her family coat of arms sort of gave it away," Maxine said, staring at the beautiful gold coat of arms that was painted on either side of the carriage. It worked almost as well as a trumpeter or herald to announce that I was riding in Marian's carriage.

"I am leaving Nightmare behind." I took a breath and managed to squeeze a few tears out of my eyes. "Thank you all so much. Your friendship will be irreplaceable in my heart."

"I hope you can visit again sometime," George sadly smiled.

"Good bye, Lady Mary," Maxine said, elegantly bowing.

"Good bye!" I called as the carriage started to roll away.

Elizabeth waved once, an elegant gesture, before wiping her eyes with a handkerchief offered to her by Edward. (If those two were not engaged by the end of the year, I would eat my hat.)

I waved until the carriage rounded a corner and my friends fell out of sight. I leaned back into my seat as the carriage picked up speed. The two bays pulling it dashed forward, their hooves clattering against the cobblestone.

Within minutes, we were out of the inner sanction of the castle and out in the open-air markets and shops. The horses thundered down the streets, neighing as the coachman called to them.

We were but a short distance from the city gate when the coachman shouted and the coach was pulled into a sharp halt, right on cue.

The coachmen yelled angrily, and I heard male voices offer several apologies.

I slid to the opposite side of the carriage and threw the door open. The carriage was nested along the side of the road, inches away from the stone walls of two shops. Directly in between the shops was a small alley, which my door swung into.

I turned out of the alley and made a sharp left turn, bounding into a tailor's shop. Marian was waiting for me inside.

"Took you long enough," she hissed, tossing me my usual Robin Hood uniform.

"Sorry," I panted, running past the tailor and his wife before I skid into their dressing room. "Thank you," I tossed over my shoulder before slamming the door shut.

The shop belonged to Robert's brother. Robert was an ex-tailor and one of my Merry Men, the one who taught me the fancy stitches. Robert's brother was a Robin Hood sympathizer and had offered his shop for my use.

I quickly shed my dress and threw on my clothes. I was pulling on a boot as I hopped out of the dressing room.

"Robyn!" a Merry Man—Tom—cried. I looked up as I flexed my foot before hurriedly walking over to Marian.

"Hello Tom, it's good to see you," I smiled, patting his back as I passed him.

He and the two other Merry Men who were with him were dressed as farmers. They had been the ones to stop the carriage, crashing a cart of vegetables directly in front of it. They were the only Merry Men in Nottingham besides Will and John. They had come with my seconds-in-commands and stayed with Robert's brother when Little John and Will Scarlet attended the ball. It was the only way they weren't caught as well.

"Hello, Lobb, Ryan." I greeted the other two men as Marian twitched a tan cape over my shoulders. I fastened it at the collar, making sure it covered my whole body before Marian slammed a helmet on my head, one that shadowed my face and covered my nose.

"Perfect. You're tall enough to be a man. Everyone will assume you're my guard. Mother has been sending those knightly lap dogs with me everywhere anyway. It's no secret that I support Robin Hood; they'll think you're my escort to keep me from running off," Marian said, wrenching the helmet so it was straight on my head. My trademark hat with the pheasant feather was already on my head, my hair pinned up beneath it. The feather stabbed my head, shoved down by the helmet.

"Ouch," I muttered, the crown of my skull stinging. "Tom, Lobb, Ryan, you know what to do?" I asked.

They nodded.

"Our disguises are in the corner," Tom said. "Thaddeus, that's Robert's brother, just filled an order for Nottingham livery uniforms. Lucky for us, there's a few extra. I'll get into the stables and get Crafty and some additional horses ready. Lobb and Ryan will take care of the gate."

"See? They know the plan. Come on, we're leaving," Marian said, shoving two long packages in my arms before storming out of the store.

I bowed to Robert's relatives. "Thank you again. We will compensate you for your troubles," I said.

Thaddeus waved a hand. "It is no problem at all. It's an *honor*," he insisted.

I settled for smiling as a reply before I bolted out of the shop, hustling after Marian. "Am I your soldier or delivery boy?" I asked, shifting the packages in my arms.

"It's the same position," Marian flippantly shrugged.

"You're a terrible person," I said as Marian led me through the winding streets, heading for Nottingham Square.

A crowd had already formed along the platform that held the gallows. Two ropes ominously swung in the breeze. I swallowed as I stared at the terrible sight.

Marian whistled between her teeth. "They're awfully anxious to get them dead and buried," she noted.

A couple villagers eagerly awaited Little John and Will Scarlet's arrival, but over half of the crowd seemed somber and dissatisfied.

"Come on. We need the height advantage," Marian said, abruptly pulling away from the crowd. I followed her up, out of the depths of the square. A gilded, golden chair was being set up in a roped off area, most likely for Prince John.

Marian led me into the castle wall, charging blindly up a winding staircase. We popped out on top of the castle wall. Soldiers closely guarded the area, walking up and down the walls like watchdogs. None of them tried to stop Marian as she plowed through their careful formations. I hastily followed her.

She took a second staircase down; this one was pressed snug against the side of the castle wall. It stopped halfway down, opening up into a shallow walkway that was just above the castle square. Strings of flags crisscrossed over our heads, and lords and ladies began to gather around the chair meant for Prince John.

"Are you ready?" Marian asked, waving to her parents, who were seated in chairs on the ground.

"Yes," I said with a steadiness I did not feel.

Marian chuckled. "Nervous?"

"Of course, but this isn't a simple robbing job. Their lives are on the line. I won't fail," I vowed.

"I believe it," Marian said, turning to smile at me while running a finger across the bridge of her aquiline nose.

George swept onto the scene and climbed the platform to inspect the gallows. I straightened, the packages in my arms nearly toppling over. If George was here, the Sheriff wouldn't be far behind.

Sure enough, minutes later, trumpets sounded and the Royal carriage pulled into the town square. Prince John exited it, and the Sheriff dismounted the horse he had ridden behind the carriage. The two made it through the crowd with their excessively large squad of soldiers. The prince seated himself in his seat, the Sheriff standing at his side.

The crowd shifted and murmured to each other, and I carefully set the packages down before I stood.

The Sheriff coughed once before baaing away in his sheep-like voice. "My liege, Prince John, you are here to witness the death of John Little, also known as Little John, and William Gamwell, who was the Earl of Maxfield before his title fell from the family, who now goes by the name of Will Scarlet. Both men are traitors to the crown and to England, and serve the cutthroat outlaw, Robin Hood."

The Prince cleared his voice before shouting, "Bring out the prisoners!" His voice broke halfway through the command.

Four trumpets sounded, and the crowd started to yell. Some screamed insults, others cheered. Eventually twelve soldiers broke into view. Will and John were held in the center, blindfolded and bound.

I squatted down and carefully ripped open the packages, discreetly pushing back the layers and layers of cloth. I smiled when I unfolded the last layer of material, revealing a beautiful longbow, a quiver, and my horn. I stood and kicked the cloth back over the weapons, staring down at the castle square with a blank face when Little John and Will Scarlet passed beneath us.

They looked like sheep being led to the slaughter.

The Sheriff was still baaing away, listing all of the wrongs my men had supposedly committed. "For robbing and attacking the persons of several lords, for plundering and stealing from the Royal carriage and assaulting His Royal Majesty, Prince John, for wrongfully disguising themselves and breaking into a party for Honored Persons…."

Will and John were led up the platform, kicked when they blindly stumbled on the stairs. Unable to watch, I cut my eyes over to Marian's parents. Oddly, George and Maxine were standing next to them, talking to each other in lowered voices.

"Robyn," Marian gently called, reaching out to squeeze my wrist.

"For assisting and serving the outlaw Robin Hood, for killing numerous deer belonging to the King..." the Sheriff droned on.

Marian continued, "It's time for me to leave. I can't be here when you shoot."

I nodded. "Thank you, Marian."

"What are friends for?" She winked.

I moved to release her hand and began to head back to the bow and arrow.

"Ouch," Marian jerked to a stop. "Hold on, my ring is caught on your sleeve."

I turned back around. "I'll get it. You'll just make it worse," I said, carefully sliding my hand in between the material of my shirt and her hand. I tugged on her ring, freeing my shirt.

"And for the destruction of several prison cells," the Sheriff wryly continued. (Will and John must have played rough in the dungeons.) The soldiers slipped the nooses around Will and John's necks.

Marian smiled at me, her blue eyes swimming with worry.

"It'll be fine," I promised.

"Oh, Robyn," Marian said, reaching out to quickly hug me before she scampered off, glancing back only once.

"I hear by sentence the rogues Will Gamwell and John Little... to *death*!" the Sheriff shouted.

The crowd howled and cheered, their shouts rising to a volume I didn't think possible.

I hastily swept up the quiver and the bow before nocking an arrow, training it on Little John.

I vaguely noted that Marian's parents and George were watching me with horror. Maxine tipped his head, as though trying to figure out what was going on. He didn't get it. He didn't know what Marian's parents and George already did. I was Robin Hood, and I was here to save my men.

George spun on his heels and shouted, waving his arms at the Sheriff, but the roar of the crowd drowned out his voice.

Instead, one of the soldiers moved to pull the lever that would make the wooden floor drop out beneath Will and John. I shot off one arrow, successfully snapping the rope hanging over John's head. An instant later, I shot a second arrow, which took care of Will's noose, freeing both of my men right before the lever was pulled.

Little John and Scarlet fell straight through the opened hole in the platform. The crowd roared, but George had reached the Sheriff. Together, they stared at me with shock.

"A Hood! A Hood! A Hood!" some of the villages began to chant.

I whipped off the helmet, praying my hair wouldn't slide out of my pheasant feather cap, and pulled the cape off my shoulders. I lifted my ivory horn to my lips and blew once before I fixed my longbow on my back. I jumped and caught a string of flags overhead. I sawed at the rope with the edge of an arrow and snapped it. I fixed my grip before leaping off the shallow walkway. I flew through the air, heading directly for the platform, which soldiers were starting to pile onto.

The Sheriff bellowed, but his bleating was covered up by the crowd, which was now mostly overpowering cheers.

I plowed at least three soldiers off the platform before I managed to skid to a stop. I released the string of banners and started whacking soldiers in the gut with my bow.

Will Scarlet popped out of the hole in the platform, standing on Little John's shoulders.

"Robyn!" he shouted.

He helped Little John out before the duo started cracking heads.

The thundering of horses swept away the roar of the crowd, and in flew Tom with several dozen horses. The horses plowed through the crowd, rampaging and bowling over any who got in their way.

"I thought you said *some* horses, not a stable!" I shouted to my

Merry Man as I pushed a soldier off the platform and into the panicked crowd.

"Not my fault!" Tom insisted. "It was your demon horse! Be grateful I managed to get him tacked up!"

"Little John, Will! We're getting out of here!" I called, running to Crafty, who had reared onto his hind legs, planted his front legs on the platform, and was biting a soldier in the calf.

"Coming!" Little John cheerfully said, literally picking up a soldier and throwing him over his head.

Crafty released the soldier and fell back to all four legs. I hopped on him and gathered up the reins.

Little John thundered across the platform and threw himself on a tacked up chestnut behind Crafty.

Will Scarlet slowly worked his way across the platform, fighting soldiers with a sword he had taken off a fallen man.

"*Will!*" I shouted. "*Now!*"

"Yes, Robyn!" Will cheerfully shouted. A few seconds later, he flew off the platform, landing on the remaining saddled horse.

"Go, go, *go!*" I shouted, heeling Crafty. My black horse took off like a streak, leading the way through the streets.

Soldiers tried to follow us, but the horses that were liberated from stable were still galloping around, causing mass chaos as villagers fled and screamed.

We tore down the streets, our horses clattering across the cobblestone road.

"The gates are down, we'll never get out!" Little John shouted.

"We'll get out!" I promised before Crafty jumped a vegetable stand.

Within minutes, we were galloping up to the main gate. "Lobb! Ryan!" I shouted as Crafty reared and wickedly neighed.

The air was filled with the clanging bells, and trumpeting horses and screaming villagers could still be heard from the castle square. But over all of this clatter, I could still hear my blessed men.

"*We can't find the switch that will toggle the bridge!*" Lobb shouted.

"*Silence! Do you want to call soldiers in here?*" Ryan yelled.

"*No, but what's this??*" Lobb loudly asked.

"*Wha—don't touch that!*" Ryan screamed.

"*What?*" Lobb asked.

"*DON'T touch that!*" Ryan shouted.

"*I can't understand you. Repeat yourself, please!*" Lobb requested.

"*I SAID…noooooo,*" Ryan shrieked.

The wooden drawbridge dropped like a sack of flour, shaking the ground when it landed.

"YOU IDIOT!" Ryan screamed as our horses neighed and shied away from the suddenly open gate.

"Well, the gates are open," Little John helpfully pointed out.

"RYAN, LOBB! COME ON!" I shouted.

Two soldiers hurried out of the empty gate house, practically falling down the stairs. The taller one, Lobb, hurtled in my direction. I gave him a hand up, and he flopped onto Crafty's back. After Ryan mounted up behind Tom, we urged our horses forward again.

Our horses carefully picked their way across the drawbridge. Some of the wooden boards had snapped in places, and it pitifully creaked as we crossed. When we reached the open road I gave Crafty his head. He snorted as we fled Nottingham Castle, leaving chaos in our wake.

4

SUDDEN CONFESSIONS

We crossed the open plain between Nottingham Castle and Sherwood Forest with ease. I pulled Crafty into a walk and spun him around. No one was following us, but a bunch of soldiers were standing around the drawbridge with obvious dismay.

I couldn't help it. The heroicness of the moment caught up with me.

I unstrapped my horn from my side and blew one long, *smug* note before directing Crafty back into the forest.

Behind me, Lobb whooped and shouted. "That's my Robin Hood, Sheriff! And he's got yer goat!"

Eventually Tom joined in, hollering and singing no tune in particular. Ryan watched the two with a pinched expression and laughed only when Tom was nearly knocked out of the saddle by a wayward branch.

Operating out of habit, Crafty and I nearly led the group to our main camp in Sherwood before I finally snapped out of my fit of joy.

"Halt!" I shouted, pulling back on the reins. Crafty locked his legs and skid to a stop, the horses behind us scrambled to avoid smacking into Crafty.

The singing Lobb slipped right off Crafty's back, and Will Scarlet barely avoided running him over.

"What, what is it?" Tom shouted.

"What's wrong?" Little John added.

"Bloody hell, Robyn, you could warn us next time," Will Scarlet chided.

"Robin, what happened?" Ryan asked.

"Ow," Lobb said from the ground. His eyes nearly popped out of his head when Crafty set a hoof down next to his head.

"I almost forgot," I said, twisting in the saddle, ignoring Lobb's whimpers. "I'm not coming back."

"*What?*"

"Not coming back?"

"But Robyn, you *have* to!"

I ignored Tom, Ryan, and Lobb and kept my gaze fixed on Little John and Will, who had moved their horses back behind Crafty.

Will Scarlet uncomfortably shifted, but Little John nodded at the other three Merry Men. "Tom, Ryan, Lobb. Head back to camp," he said. "We'll see you there in a bit."

"We don't take orders from you," Ryan snarled.

Tom turned in his saddle to shake his head at Ryan in a warning before pulling his horse alongside Little John's. "If you don't bring her back, we'll feed you to the wolves," he warned in a quiet voice before brightening. "Right then! Come along Lobb, let's get moving!" he said before heeling his horse.

"Wait up!" Lobb complained, picking himself off the ground before lamely trotting after the riding pair. "I haven't a horse! You'll have to slow down!"

"Why should we, you silly gawp fish?" Tom laughed.

"I am *not* silly! It was I who opened up the gates!" Lobb protested, crashing through the woods after them.

"No, you *destroyed* the gate," Ryan said.

The trio eventually fell out of my hearing range, leaving me with Little John and Scarlet.

"Robyn... you have to come back. You have to lead us," Little John said after several moments of forest-y silence.

Crafty arched his neck and chewed his bit. I was silent.

"We need you, Robyn. We can't get by without you," Will Scarlet evenly said.

"But you said—" I started.

"Forget what we said!" Will Scarlet exploded.

Little John rubbed his forehead with a giant hand before reaching down to stroke his horse's neck. "We were being fools, Robyn. *I* was being a fool. A wretched fool. The contest was unfair and I knew it. I just wanted—" he broke off for a second. "I just. I, I was stupid Robyn. Please forgive us. Forgive me."

I wheeled Crafty around so I could properly face them. "Whether you were being foolish or not isn't the question. You legitimately beat me, and said you wanted to lead the Merry Men. Who am I to stop you?" I asked, gesturing with my free hand. (I didn't dare release Crafty's reins; there was no telling what the demon horse would do.)

"Robyn, you don't understand! It wasn't that I didn't want you as a leader anymore," Little John said.

"It is the same for me. I would never see you replaced," Will Scarlet echoed.

"Then explain to me, Little John, and Will Scarlet, why you demanded that Little John should be our leader? Make me understand what you *really* meant by that. Please, enlighten me," I hissed.

Crafty, sensing my foul mood, pinned his ears and snarled at the duo.

Scarlet and Little John avoided my gaze and stared down at their hands.

I blinked back tears. So in the end, they couldn't even explain themselves. If they couldn't do that much, then surely they still didn't want me as their leader. The two men I had trusted the most betrayed me. And it hurt deeply.

"That's what I thought," I said, trying to keep my tears in and the hurt from lacing my voice. I clucked to Crafty, who rocked forward into a walk. We snaked between the mounted Little John and Will Scarlet, moving past them.

We were almost out of sight when Little John called out. "Robyn! Wait!"

"Robyn!" Scarlet shouted.

The two barreled up to me on their horses.

"It was us," Little John said in a rushed, jumble of words when they caught up. "I started it. I thought you would like me more since I was your right hand man. I was here first. If you were to love either of us, it should be me," Little John said, scowling at Will.

Scarlet interrupted him as they swiveled their horses in front of mine, making us stop. "Much and Will Stutely told us they would never see you married until the Merry Men were pardoned and disbanded, and you were no longer the outlawed leader. We couldn't very well get you pardoned, but it occurred to Little John that he could unseat you, which might be close enough."

"So I challenged you to an unfair contest. I figured in the morning, we could talk it over and you would choose one of us and… and," Little John trailed off. "I didn't think things through very well," he admitted.

"I'm afraid I don't understand," I said, rapidly blinking. "All of this was because Much and Will Stutely said they won't let me be married?"

Little John and Will Scarlet swapped glances before turning to me and speaking in one voice.

"Robyn, we love you."

"*Really* love you," Scarlet stressed.

"Not the way the rest of the Merry Men love you," Little John added.

"We *really* love you," Will Scarlet repeated.

"So choose one of us."

I couldn't tell which one of them said that in such a pleading voice, and I wasn't sure I wanted to know.

I stared at them, completely dumbfounded. My mind was blanking. Their sudden, simultaneous confessions were the last things I ever expected to hear in my entire *life*. Besides the infamously flirtatious Dan the Musician, I had never been paid any particular attention by men as handsome, comely, and powerful as John and Will. (And Will was a lord's son. A LORD'S *son*.)

I was so stupefied my hands went slack. Crafty judged his moment of liberation was near, and threw me without apology. I went flying off his back when he crow hopped, cracking into a small tree.

As I groaned, blinking stars out of my eyes while trying to regain my knocked out breath, Crafty nickered under his horsey breath and started meandering through Sherwood, heading back for camp.

"Robyn!" Scarlet cried as he and Little John slid off their horses and rushed to my side.

"I'm fine," I groaned, already disengaging myself from the tree. "I'm fine," I repeated, standing up on shaky legs.

When I finally reoriented myself, I realized both of the men were clasping my elbows. Naturally shied by the awkward situation, I shook them off before abruptly plunging through the woods, heading for camp.

"I must return to camp," I muttered, scrambling over a log. Maybe if I ignored them, they would go away.

Unfortunately, Little John and Will Scarlet trailed after me, leading their horses by the reins.

"Robyn?" Little John hesitantly called.

I stopped and turned around to stare at the pair.

They shifted and looked a little uncomfortable.

"We—" Scarlet started.

I abruptly slapped my hands over my ears. "La-la-la-la-la! I can't hear you!" I declared, spinning back around as my face turned the most brilliant shade of red. "La-la-la!" I shouted while skirting around a bush, following the unseen trails of the Merry Men.

Little John gave me the fright of a lifetime when he suddenly grasped my left wrist and pulled my hand off my ear. "Reacting like a bashful child isn't going to make this situation disappear, Robyn."

I removed my right hand from my ear only so I could properly elbow Little John in the gut, making the unsuspecting man bend over in a gasp.

I squirmed away from him and started tearing through the underbrush. "Marian! You're never around when I need you!" I shouted, careening through the underbrush. Marian would know what to do in these circumstances.

I hurriedly cleared the last natural wall of trees that hedged in our camp, knocking a scout clean off his feet.

"Sorry," I said, looking down at the fallen Merry Man.

"Robyn?" a familiar voice asked.

My eyes shot up and I spotted Much and Will Stutely halfway across the camp.

My face scrunched up and I tore towards them. "Much! Will!" I wailed, throwing myself at them.

Much caught me and had to be steadied by Will Stutely to keep from falling over.

"Robyn, you're back!" Will Stutely crowed, joyful as ever.

"What's wrong?" Much asked, running a soothing hand up and down my back.

At that moment, Little John and Will Scarlet entered our camp, still towing their stolen horses behind them.

I tightened the hold my fists had on Much's shirt, which did not go unnoticed by my original Merry Man as he stared across the camp.

"You didn't," he called to Scarlet and Little John, his voice dripping with disgust.

The duo of Robyn Lovers swapped guilty glances.

"By Mary the beloved mother, what on earth *possessed* you to tell her?" Much growled.

"You *knew?*" I squeaked into Much's shirt.

"You two are proper fools!" Will Stutely chimed in.

"Well, at least it brought her back," Will Scarlet pointed out.

Much scowled and slowly spun around, twirling me with him. "Come on, Robyn. You must want something to eat."

I knew an opening for a total retreat when I saw one. "Actually," I quietly ventured. "I probably need to sleep," I said, pulling away from Much, baiting my male nursemaid.

Will Stutely blinked. "It's barely noon."

"It is," I agreed. "But I stayed up the whole night with Marian while we mapped out the plan to rescue Little John and Scarlet."

The camp was utterly silent for several moments.

"What?" Much asked, his voice iron hard.

"Pardon?" I innocently blinked. (There were times when I could use Much and Will Stutely's mother hen characteristics to my advantage.)

Will Stutely gently took my arm and carted me off to my hut while Much spun on his heels to glare at Will Scarlet and Little John.

"Come along, Robyn. It's probably best if you go to bed," Will said in a sing-song voice, smiling at the excited Merry Men who were clambering around, grinning at me.

"Okay," I agreed, pausing when I got to my hut. "It's good to be home," I said before opening the door. My room was still neat and tidy. I flopped on my bed and fell asleep within a minute.

I slept the whole day through and didn't wake up until just before dawn the following morning. When I stumbled out of my hut, in something of a daze, Marian was sitting on a log, rubbing morning dew off a piece of grass.

"Finally, here you are. Really, I expected you to be unfit to sleep with your mind racing about those daring declarations Little John and Will Scarlet made," she said, standing up before brushing off her full skirts.

I groaned. "Don't remind me," I pleaded as I staggered pass her. "I already feel as though I were run down by the Sherriff's men. I don't need reality to set in any sooner than possible. What are you doing here? You never rise this early. Not to mention, your parents surely must be keeping you under lock and key after yesterday's adventure."

"As you mentioned, I never get up this early. My parents didn't bother to post guards underneath my window at this hour. It would be positively ridiculous. No, the only thing that could drag me out of my warm, comfortable, feather bed, Robyn dear, is you," Marian answered, following me to one of the campfires.

"Me? What about me?" I groggily asked as I plopped down and added a few logs to the fire after peering into a pot of oatmeal one of my men was preparing.

A scant number of Merry Men were already up, tending to the fires and getting breakfast ready. The rest of the brood wouldn't turn out until the sun's rays started to peek above the horizon.

"Last night, I received a message from Much, claiming that Scarlet and Little John have bewitched you and you were so frightened, just like a helpless woodland creature," Marian said, rolling her eyes as I took a wooden spoon from a passing Merry Man and thumped it into the pot of oatmeal. "Naturally, I judged the letter to be written in a hysterical manner, which is easy to nudge Much into, but if my guess is right, Little John and Will Scarlet have finally told you they're in love with you," Marian said as she settled down at next to me. I nearly lost the spoon in the oatmeal at her blunt report.

"Um, well, erm," I sputtered.

"So they did," Marian concluded.

I leaned the spoon against the lip of the pot and turned to my best friend. "What am I going to do, Marian?"

"It all depends on you, Robyn. Do you love either of them?" she prodded.

I stood and started pacing, my eyebrows furrowing. "Of course I love *both* of them. They're my right hand men, Marian. I trust them just as much as I trust Much, and Will Stutely, and *you!*"

"Could you love either one of them as something more?" Marian calmly inquired, ignoring my pacing.

It struck me as being rather odd that *Marian*, out of all people, was investigating my feelings of love.

"I don't know, maybe. I mean, they're both so—but, not right now!" I declared, suddenly halting. One of the very quiet Merry Men who was trying to get breakfast ready nearly rammed into me. He froze and did a very decent impression of a rock before slowly edging off, clearly not wanting to be included in this type of discussion.

I didn't blame him.

"Robyn. Maid Marian," he muttered before hurrying off to another fire.

"What do you mean by not now?" Marian asked, ignoring the interruption.

I settled back on my heels and scrunched my nose. "Now is hardly the time to be falling in love, even if I did fancy either one of them. I'm leading dozens of men in the art of robbery. I've made countless men into cunning outlaws. I'm trying to keep them from getting caught by the idiot Sheriff, not to mention the actual brains behind his operation, George, and, to top it all off, Prince John! Best yet, I have to somehow gather enough money to set King Richard free. No, this is *not* the time to be thinking of love."

"So it's just temporary? One day you might consider them?" Marian asked.

I shuddered, dreading the day I would have to face my men like that again. It was embarrassing, and it made my entire world heave. To think that *they* would like someone like me—I cut the thought off.

"Yes," I replied. "The day Robin Hood and his Merry Men are no longer necessary I will think about their… confessions."

Marian nodded once before standing and calling out. "Did you hear that, boys?"

"Loud and clear," Little John said, stepping out from behind a hut.

"It is an agreeable solution," Will Scarlet said, materializing next to my fire. "Little John and I were being impatient. We should have never brought it up in the first place…but it was the only way to explain everything."

"All that matters is that Robyn said no," Much announced, following Little John to my fire.

"For now," Little John amended.

Much ignored him. "Let's forget all of this foolishness. The contest, Little John and Scarlet's asinine arrest, their confessions, everything."

"For now," Little John repeated.

"You were *listening in*? This was a set up!" I realized, leaping to my feet. "Marian, you betrayed me!" I shouted.

Marian shrugged. "They would never believe anything I said unless they heard it fall from your lips. Would you have rather told them face to face than tell me and have them *happen* to overhear?"

I winced as I thought about that possibility. "No," I sighed.

"So let's celebrate. Robyn is back, everyone is safe, and it's breakfast time," Will Stutely said, appearing with a pack of Merry Men.

I smiled, mildly moved but above all, relieved to be leaving the topic of love behind me. "Of course. I am Robin Hood and you are my band of Merry Men. Let us be merry!" I shouted.

All of the Merry Men had turned out of their beds by this point, and most of them shouted and raised their arms in agreement.

After several seconds of shouting, the Merry Men split up to do the morning chores. I was about to investigate the whereabouts of my longbow and quiver, but Marian grabbed me by the elbow.

"Walk with me," she bid. "It's dawn, I need to be getting home soon."

I complied, and together we trailed over to the pen that held the Pony, Crafty, the new horses stolen from Nottingham, and a still saddled Nearly Dead.

"What's on your mind?" I asked as Marian ducked in the pen to snag her horse.

Marian turned around to consider me for a moment before speaking. "I'm coming to live with you and the Merry Men."

I was statue still for a moment before reacting. "What? Are you mad?! You can't, Marian. Sherwood is hardly the place for a lady. I don't care how robust you are, you are a being of nobility and power. You *can't* stay here, Marian."

"I'm coming," Marian stubbornly refuted. "I can't stand living in that castle any longer with the odious Sir Guy of Gisborne constantly nipping at my heels like an accursed lap dog! Not to mention my father and mother, pandering to the Sheriff and Prince John. I cannot stand it any longer Robyn. I *must* leave. I can survive in the woods just as well as your other Merry Men!"

"It's not a matter of surviving, Marian," I said in a pleading voice as she swung onto Nearly Dead's back. "We need you out there. You are our main source of information and supplies! The only way we hear credible information about the Prince or King Richard is through you! We need you right where you are."

Marian looked unconvinced.

"Just wait," I pleaded as I swung the wooden fence open. "I'll come to you tomorrow. Somehow. I'll break in. We can talk."

"Fine," Marian frostily agreed. "But you better show up, Robyn. Otherwise I'm riding back here with as many supplies as I can carry, and I won't return home until King Richard is back on the throne," Marian vowed before heeling Nearly Dead. The grey mare took off, tearing out of the camp.

I shut the fence behind Marian's speedy exit before I rubbed my eyes with my hands.

"Did something happen?" Will Scarlet asked.

"Did something happen to Marian?" Little John asked.

I jumped, startled by their sudden appearance. "Umm," I uttered. They continued to stare at me with open, reasonable expressions.

Apparently they would be following Much's orders and would pretend like nothing happened. I felt relieved, but at the same time, I was having a hard time looking at them the same way.

"Robyn, are you even listening?" Will Scarlet teased, one of his eyebrows quirking up.

"Yes," I said, sheepishly itching the back of my head. "Yes, something happened with Marian. She's decided to make things even more complicated than they already are," I said before nervously laughing and striding off.

I would have to get over their silly confessions. I *needed* to.

5

ALAN-A-DALE

True to my word, the following day I found myself wandering through Sherwood, wearing one of the dresses I had snagged and improved upon during my stay at Nottingham castle.

I did not take Crafty or the pony. My plan was to waltz up to Marian's castle— dressed as a passable female—and sneak my way to Marian's quarters.

I had a terrible time convincing Much and Will Stutely to let me go meet her. In the end, they only consented as long as I left Little John and Will Scarlet behind. (I suspected that duo was going to get the lecture of a lifetime in my absence.) Honestly, I was a little glad to be alone. Things were still a bit awkward between the three of us.

I ambled through the forest, silent in spite of my heavy skirts, aiming for a worn path I knew of that wormed around the edges of Sherwood Forest before swirling over to Marian's castle.

During my walk, I heard a male voice... singing. For a split second, I feared one of my Merry Men would magically appear and haul me off to enter some sort of fight against the singing stranger, as they were prone to do. But after several tense seconds, I relaxed and recalled I was alone.

Curiosity getting the better part of me, I angled my path towards the singing voice. If I was lucky, maybe it was a fat lord with an equally fat purse, trying to lull a gentle lady.

The closer I got to the singing, the more I appreciated the joyful song. The unnamed singer was clearly a great musician. (Not at all like Dan!)

I slowed down as I neared the voice, lurking among the trees and bushes to inspect the singer. It was a young lad; he had to be my age or younger. He was comely, and as he strolled through my forest, he trailed his fingers across the harp strings and sang like a lark.

Instantly I knew he was neither rich nor intelligent. The blasted boy didn't carry a single weapon on his person, much less a purse. All he had was his harp, which he played prettily enough to make the King's minstrels jealous.

I made up my mind to leave the poor boy be. He was obviously a cheerful, if not oblivious soul. I had no quarrel with him, I could only hope he kept to the outskirts of Sherwood and didn't venture closer to my camp. (Because then surely my men would force me into some kind of musical match against him, just to spite me.)

I abruptly plunged through the trees, half startling the singing boy.

He spun around and nearly bolted, but paused when he caught sight of me. He smiled but continued his song, quickly falling out of sight as I hurried to Huntingdon Castle.

Sneaking into the castle was easier than I ever previously remembered. Maybe it was because I had earned nerves of steel after chatting so much with George, or maybe it was because I had finally garnered enough experience with full skirts that I could walk without tripping.

I sashayed through the gates of Huntingdon, and the guards on duty gave me only an appreciative secondary glance.

Once inside, I navigated my way through the town section before sneaking through the inner walls, walking with a band of washing maids. I broke off from them at the stables and boldly walked around it, heading for the gardens.

None of the guards stopped me, or even appeared to be suspicious of me, a single lady wandering around without a chaperone or friend at her side. I got to the gardens without a hitch, and I was soon sitting on a bench reflectively staring at the castle keep. I had never been to Marian's room; I didn't know where it was, much less how to get inside.

"Lady Mary?"

I twisted and peered over a rose bush. Marian was smiling at me with her pretty, blue eyes. "Why, Lady Marian. How good it is to see you," I greeted, standing up.

"And how good it is to see you! Come, we must catch up. Tell me how the Gamwells fare," Marian invited, holding out her arm.

I looped my arm through hers, as I often did with Elizabeth, and Marian yanked me around the garden. We traveled down a well-worn path, popping out by the kitchens. Marian pulled me inside, immersing us with the servants. We were pushed forward like lily pads on a pond before Marian wrangled us out of the bustling kitchens and into a narrow hallway.

"Your room is situated in a very strange place, Lady Marian," I laughed in a warning tone.

"Shh," Marian urged, taking a turn down a twisting hall. She stopped outside a wooden door, opened it, and pushed me in before shutting it behind her. "We can talk freely here. This is just an extra storage room. No one comes this way."

"How reassuring," I muttered, glancing around the dust filled room. All that was in it were crates, barrels, and some rolled up rugs.

Marian frowned. "My room is positively flocked with

babbling ladies maids. We could never talk there. You're just lucky I was able to pull myself away without being noticed."

"Why the extra security?" I asked, plopping down on a dusty crate. "Did they catch you yesterday morning?"

"No, worse. Prince John has been making noises that Sir Guy of Gisborne is in need of a wife," Marian sighed.

"So?" I shrugged.

"I'm the perfect candidate for that unlucky position," Marian said as she started to pace. "Father and Mother are extremely upset that I'm blatantly supporting you. It's hurting their standing with Prince John. That's why marrying me off to one of his favorite knights would solidify the relationship. The only reason Father didn't immediately agree is because he's not yet completely under my mother's thumb, who is all for it, and because Sir Guy is drop-dead broke."

"But Prince John isn't going to be our ruler forever. You'll be sunk when King Richard returns," I objected.

"I *know*, but the talk is that King Richard *isn't* going to return. Face it, Robyn, you and the Merry Men are the only ones who are seriously raising money to free him. Even his own supporters, like my father, don't dare move with Prince John breathing down their necks."

"We'll get the ransom. And I won't let them marry you off to Sir Guy," I vowed before groaning as I recalled that particular knight. "Of course he has to be the only competent knight Prince John's brought with him. Otherwise I could just challenge him to a duel and off him, but I'm not willing to take that chance with Sir Guy," I said, sucking on my lip.

"Don't worry about it. I've decided—I'm coming back to Sherwood with you," Marian shrugged, stopping in front of my crate.

"No you aren't, Marian," I sharply said.

"Yes I am, Robyn! You don't get how horrible this is!" Marian snarled, reaching out to shake my shoulders.

"Bear with it, Marian. You are our only source of information in such a high level of nobility. We *need* you here. I'll go back to Sherwood and talk things over with the Merry Men. We'll calculate how much more we need to free King Richard and figure out something to end this Sir Guy business. You can expect my return in two or three days," I said, standing up.

Marian backed away as I brushed dust off my dress. "You promise?" she sulked.

"Promise. I'll come up with a plan," I said, meeting her gaze with my own sharp brown eyes. "You're a part of my company, too. I won't throw you to the dogs."

"Whenever did you grow to become so heroic?" Marian sighed, reaching out to hug me.

"You have no one but yourself to blame for that one. This is your Outlaw Dream. You made me into Robin Hood," I winked.

"I did, didn't I?" Marian wondered, her forehead wrinkling.

"Come now, you had better get back before your cackling guard hens realize you've flown the coop," I said, starting for the door.

"The same goes for you. How on earth did you procure Much's permission to leave the camp?"

"I did a lot of swindling," I said, opening the door.

"I bet," Marian snorted behind me.

WITHIN TWO HOURS, I was back at my camp in Sherwood, trading the dress for my more desirable lincoln green uniform.

"What did Marian have to say?" Much asked, waiting for me outside my hut.

"Nothing good, that is for certain," I called through the door, straightening my green hose before grabbing my pheasant feather cap, placing it on my head. I threw the door open with a bang. "She wants to come live with us in Sherwood."

Much grew violently pale, while behind him, Will Stutely turned green. Will Scarlet's color remained normal, but he inexplicably gained four wrinkles on his forehead. Similarly, Little John snapped the bow he was trying to mend.

"What did you say?" Little John carefully asked, seated in front of a fire a short distance away from my hut.

I left my room, closing the door behind me. "Her mother and the prince have plans to marry her off to Sir Guy of Gisborne, that odiously pompous knight who was riding with Prince John when we robbed him," I explained, walking up to Little John's fire.

"The one with the bad haircut?" Much recalled.

"That would be him," Will Scarlet agreed. "Little John and I got a good look at him in Nottingham Castle. I can't believe Maid Marian's father would let her marry such a fop. He's not a knight, he's bloody broke!"

"Says the earl who lives in the forest like a common squatter," Will Stutely piped in.

Will Scarlet shot him a glare.

"Lobb," I called.

"Yes, Robyn?" Lobb asked from the edge of camp. He was returning from guard duty.

"Go with Tom and get Friar Tuck. Tell him his assistance is required."

"Yes, Robyn!" Lobb hummed before disappearing off into the woods.

"What do we need Friar Tuck for?" Much asked. "I thought you finally gave up saying your last rites before every robbery we pull."

"This is about King Richard's ransom. If I recall correctly, Marian said he was being held for 150,000 marks. Unfortunately when we rob, we don't just get solid coins. We have gold and gems as well. I'm hoping Friar Tuck will help us get those valued and switched. Better yet, he may be able to find others who are trying to free King Richard. He's connected with our band, but he *is* a priest. Even Prince John would think twice before killing one of God's men," I said. "Much, Stutely. Could you start to gather up the gold? We're going to count it."

"Right," Will Stutely nodded.

"Sure thing, Robyn," Much agreed, casting a wary glance at Little John and Will Scarlet.

"What will we do about Marian?" Will Scarlet prompted.

I rubbed my forehead. "I'm still trying to figure that out." I paused for a moment. "It would almost be easier to get enough money to free King Richard from his prison rather than try to dissuade Sir Guy of Gisborne against Marian."

Little John snorted and Scarlet chuckled.

I smiled at their familiar actions. Leave it to Marian to create enough chaos that would get all of our minds off the last few days. "When I get our monetary amount amassed, I plan to visit Marian. With luck we'll be able to free King Richard within the year," I said.

"In no way would that be in time to save Marian," Little John said, moving to stand closer to me.

"Correct. But Big-Mouth-Marian will inform her father, who might possibly hold out from giving his consent before Christmas," I gambled, taking a few steps away from the tall man. I was *quite* aware of his presence after his shocking confession. I couldn't help it.

"The dashing outlaw Robin Hood needs me, or so I am told?" Friar Tuck announced, plowing through our camp with his large girth. Lobb and Tom hovered in his wake.

"Why, it is the good Friar Tuck! I did not expect you to arrive so soon," I greeted, walking up to my father-figure with a grin.

"I was on my way to visit you when these two nervous rabbits found me," Friar Tuck said, jerking his thumb over his shoulder at Lobb and Tom. "So, what causes the Bold and Brave Robin Hood to call me?" he winked, affectionately patting my head.

"It's about King Richard's ransom," I said.

"Ah," Friar Tuck acknowledged.

"I mean to figure out how much of his ransom we can pay," I said. "We need to start counting our assets and calculating this out."

Friar Tuck rubbed his chin and nodded. "I know Queen Eleanor is mustering up as many funds as she can get. I shall put my ear to the ground and see if I can't come up with a sum."

"Excellent. If we're lucky, we might find others who are hoarding up wealth for King Richard's release as well. I know most of the crusaders are camped across Europe, but surely some of Richard's agents have returned by now," I said.

"Be careful, Robyn," Friar Tuck warned. "Prince John and King Phillip of France have offered to pay Henry of the Holy Roman Emperor 80,000 marks to keep King Richard. Prince John means to keep Richard out of the country."

"Prince John is an inept tadpole," Will Scarlet declared. "The day he becomes King of England is the day I shall see our monarchy weakened."

I glared at my Merry Man. "You're already an outlaw, Will, but talking like that is sure to see you further outlawed, if that's possible."

"Even if you do speak truly," Little John agreed.

Friar Tuck laughed and rolled up the sleeves of his brown robes. "Let's take a look at your riches, shall we, Robyn?" he said, smoothing the whole thing over.

"Certainly, my dear Friar. Come this way," I said, leading the Friar through our camp.

AFTER COUNTING, guessing, approximating, and calculating, we discovered we had approximately 30,000 marks of wealth in our scattered safe house locations. It wasn't even a *third* of the ransom.

Friar Tuck left after dinner, promising to return soon with information about Queen Eleanor and her luck at raising funds. That left me to face Marian the following day with the bad news.

"Maybe I should come with you," Little John suggested as we ate breakfast the following morning. "If there are two of us, she can't kill you. There would be a witness."

"Maybe you're right," I said, popping a nut in my mouth.

"I'll come with!" Will Scarlet volunteered, sitting next to me, stirring a bowl of berries.

"No, you will not," Much said. "I'll be going. You can stay behind and teach swordsmanship to the trainees," Much decided.

"What?" Will Scarlet protested.

Much folded his arms across his chest. "I haven't been out with Robyn in *months*, it's my turn."

"Much is right," I agreed. "I promise I'll bring you with next time, Will," I said, getting off my log. "We're going disguised as a gaggle of females," I announced.

"Surely you jest. Stutely's sister does not have the facial stubble Little John sports," Much snorted.

"If we aren't dressed as ladies, you two will find some tanner, or butcher, or other potential Merry Man for me to fight and get thoroughly thrashed by. We go as women," I firmly stated.

IN THE END, we started wandering through the forest, utterly undisguised, wearing our usual lincoln green clothes. Our disguises, the black robes of nuns, were shoved in the packs that Little John carried on his back.

We headed down the same trail I had taken the previous day,

moving quietly as forest deer. It was a good thing too, or we might have unknowingly announced our presence to the singing musician/harper I ran into the day before.

Today he was not singing at all. Instead he was sitting on the ground, leaning against a rock. His shoulders were slouched, and he cradled his head in his hands.

I stopped to stare at the changed man as Much and Little John started to skirt around the small path he was sitting on.

"What's wrong with him?" I murmured, continuing to stare at him.

"What?" Little John asked, slinking back to my side.

"I saw this young lad just yesterday. He was as happy as could be. Today it appears as though his life has been wrenched from him," I said, watching the dejected harper with a curious frown.

Little John and Much swapped shrugs before walking away from me, bursting into the singer's sight.

"What are you doing?" I hissed.

They ignored me and swaggered up to the minstrel.

The minstrel looked up with sad eyes. "If you're here to rob me, I have nothing," he bluntly said.

Little John chuckled. "If we were thieves, we would not be going after such a small tidbit as you."

"We mean you no harm. For now," Much added.

"Our leader wants to enquire after you. Sh-he's over there. Come on, be a man and stand," Little John bid.

"There is nothing wrong with my legs, I can come out of the shadows on my own," I dryly announced, still hanging back in the shadows to tuck up the last few locks of my hair before I joined my Merry Men.

"I speak the truth. I really have nothing of value on me. Except this ring," the minstrel said, looking down at a simple, silver ring he held in his palm. "And you are welcome to it if you so desire. It is no longer any good to me," he bitterly sighed.

I rolled my eye as I strode up to the young boy. If this minstrel was anything like Dan the Musician, or the other singers and minstrels Marian had told me about, he was most likely being overly dramatic and was filled with creative sorrow.

"What good is a ring to you anyway?" I asked. "Some sort of birthright?" I had never heard of a minstrel with a birthright, but there is a first time for everything.

"Nay," the minstrel sadly sighed.

Little John blinked and bent over, inspecting the plain ring. "Oh, it's a wedding ring," he announced, standing up to smile at me.

I narrowed my eyes and gazed up at him. "You had better know that for a practical reason, and not because of…," I let my sentence trail off, trusting Little John would know I was alluding to the unspeakable confession incident.

"Nope. We've stolen plenty of them off Maid Marian's potential swains," Little John smiled.

I started breathing once again before turning back to the minstrel, who seemed to be unable to keep his neck from drooping. "See now, young minstrel. What on earth is wrong with you? Yesterday you were singing like a lark, today you are as dumpy as a vulture and carrying around a wedding ring. What happened?"

The minstrel finally looked up at me and blinked. "You saw me yesterday? But I was out here alone, in the woods. I only saw a single maid pass through here before I returned home."

"Erm," I brightly said. Mayhap he wasn't as clueless and stupid as I had originally suspected.

"Truthfully, my life was perfect then. Ellen was going to marry me," the minstrel said, growing sad again.

"Oh, so she changed her mind?" Much callously asked, scratching his scalp.

"No!" The minstrel said, bursting to his feet. "Her parents are making her marry an old windbag of a knight! They said I'm only a minstrel, I couldn't possibly provide for her. Which is true, compared to a knight I…." The harper broke off in a sigh.

"She probably changed her mind," Little John whispered to Much who nodded in consent.

I elbowed Little John before turning back to the harper. "What is your name?" I kindly asked.

"Alan-A-Dale," he replied.

"Well Alan-A-Dale, you are in luck. It just so happens that today I feel the need to reunite lovers and save fair maidens who are being unwillingly married," I announced.

"Hoping to soften Marian's heart with tales of your heroic acts?" Little John asked. "It won't work. She's not really what you would call a romantic soul."

"So it is you then!" Alan-A-Dale cried. "You are the good outlaw Robin Hood! Then you can only be Little John, and you are...," the minstrel fell silent when his eyes landed on Much, who was quite obviously not the scarlet-clad Will Scarlet who usually finished the trio.

"Much," Much supplied with a pinched expression. "Her first Merry Man."

"You are Much the miller's son! Robin Hood's greatest and most experienced Merry Man! I never thought I would live to meet such well known heroes!" Alan-A-Dale said, recovering and reacting so splendidly Much couldn't help but forgive the minstrel for not recognizing him on sight.

I smiled as Alan-A-Dale turned his attention back to me. "Then were you the fair maiden yesterday? You make a beautiful lady," he earnestly complimented me.

"Ah-um. Er," I uncomfortably shifted.

"I have no gift I can give you for the feat you are about to perform for me... but I will serve you for the rest of my days, Robin Hood," Alan-A-Dale continued, kneeling at my feet.

This made me smile in genuine happiness. "That is good to hear Alan-A-Dale. For you never know when I might need the services of a harper," I said, winking at the young man. "Now, where is this sweetheart of yours? Is she being held in a tower?" I asked. Marian's wild stories were starting to rub off on me.

"Nay," the minstrel replied. "Soon she will be at the church, which is but five miles from this place. Her parents are marrying her off today."

"Is that so," I said as I looked Alan-A-Dale up and down. I was an inch or two taller than him, but as long as I wore my boots no one would notice the shortness in my hose. "I shall go ahead in disguise. You, Alan-A-Dale, will return to my camp in Sherwood with Much and Little John," I said before turning to my accompanying Merry Men, who were already starting to object. "I need you two to go and gather twenty Merry Men and Friar Tuck. When I blow my horn during the ceremony, come to my side."

"Heavens no," Much refused at the same time Little John spoke.

"You'll be disguised?"

"Yes," I replied to my second in command's question. "I'll go in Alan's clothes and be a harper or minstrel."

Much made more noises of disbelief while Little John rubbed his chin.

"It might work. Your face is fine so you'll look young enough for your high singing voice. But you should take Much with you," he concluded.

"Agreed," I said, knowing this was probably the best deal I was going to get out of the pair. "Alright, Alan-A-Dale. Let's switch clothes," I said, turning to the young minstrel.

He was horrified. "I could *never* wear Robin Hood's clothes."

"Which is good because we wouldn't let you," Little John rumbled. "He can wear one of the nun robes until we get him back in camp and kitted up with a Sherwood uniform."

I shrugged off my quiver and handed it to Much, who would have to carry my weapons for me. "As you wish. But he had best start stripping," I said, removing my large hunting knife from the sheath strapped to my side.

"And he will. Out of your sight," Much said, pushing me out of the small copse.

Alan's clothes were red, almost the same scarlet shade of Will Scarlet's. The red hose was fine as long as I wore my boots. However, his ruffled shirt was much too small for my…erm… chest.

"This could be a problem," I said, looking down at myself. I could button the shirt but I was clearly of the female gender with the fabric settling on my female curves.

"Sir Robin Hood, do they fit alright, heeaaaa," Alan-A-Dale coughed when Little John abruptly yanked him back by the collar of his shirt, but it was already too late. He goggled at me, clearly seeing the truth.

Much sighed and removed his brown, leather vest as he walked past the stupefied minstrel and regretful Little John. "Here. Wear my vest. Little John's would not only drown you, but since he had it colored green it would surely make you look like Father Christmas."

"Thanks," I said, sliding into the proffered clothing item. I laced it up and was quiet satisfied with the end result. I carefully placed a strip of cloth running down my stomach so my front looked more flat than slanted. Little John and Much were also satisfied after a careful inspection.

"What do you think?" I asked, bending over to pick up Alan's harp. I tucked it in the crook of one arm and lazily stroked the strings with my free hand.

"It works," Little John agreed.

"You look like Dan the Musician when he's trying to be especially smarmy," Much laughed.

"Who?" Little John asked.

"No one," I waved my hand before turning to the recovering harper. "And you, Alan-A-Dale. Are you alright with this?"

"You were an awfully beautiful lady," Alan told me, ruffling his nun robes. "A part of me wondered. But, Madame Robin

Hood, you still have my loyalty and life for as long as you can use it."

"Thank you, master harper. I hope we are able to rescue your Ellen," I stretched. "Much, we're going," I said, abruptly striding off through the forest. "Be ready, Little John."

"I will!" the giant man called back, assuring me.

6

WEDDING CRASHERS

*A*n hour or so later, Much and I found the church, which was nestled in a pleasant orchard.

"Stay out here. Out of sight," I ordered.

Much grumbled but climbed a nearby tree, perfectly blending in with the green leaves.

I took a deep breath before I strolled up the church path, humming the deepest notes I could while plucking at a few of the harp strings.

A stout churchman, who I observed to be a bishop by his robes, was opening the doors of the church. He was one of the unpleasant church fellows that I wouldn't like. He was the type to let the poor starve and keep the church coffers for himself.

He smiled at me, glancing down at my harp. "God has given you a gift of music, has he?"

"I will never discredit God," I humbly said. (Even with my extravagant robbing career in full swing, I still tried not to lie to priests. Or at least I tried not to lie to them as much as I did to everyone else.)

"Who are you, what are you doing here?" the bishop inquired.

"I am but a wandering minstrel. When walking down the road

to Nottingham, I was informed that today a wedding will be performed in this most sacred place. I decided to venture here in hopes of being able to make music for the lovely bride and groom during this joyous occasion," I said, speaking as flowery as possible while plucking a few more notes. I hoped it sounded minstrel-y.

"You are certainly welcome to the ceremony," the bishop started. "It is I who will be performing the service for my good friend and his young bride. Come, play your harp that I might hear your skills."

I smiled and Much nearly wet his pants in his tree. "I cannot, sir Bishop," I truthfully said. After all, I could only pluck a few strings and hope they sounded decent. "Where I come from, it is considered bad luck to play before the budding bride is among us," I said, finishing the speech with a hand flourish.

"We will need not wait long then. Here comes the lucky couple," the bishop said, pointing past me.

I turned around and sure enough, further up the path was an old knight who was probably my father's age. With him was a pretty girl dressed in blue with her hair down and a garland of flowers perched on the crown of her head. She could only be Ellen. Trailing behind the pair was another couple, most likely Ellen's parents.

"The guests have already been seated. Go find a place for yourself, young harper, and prepare to play," the bishop instructed before waddling down the steps to greet his friend.

I could hear Much angrily rattle the tree branches over my head. No doubt he wanted some bold, dashing comment out of me. Unfortunately he wasn't going to get any.

"Yes, sir," I cheerfully said before bounding up the stairs. I could not miss the intense stare Ellen gave me, or specifically my clothes.

Much was climbing down his tree with the nimbleness of a

cat. He glared at me and pointed to the chatting bishop and knight, clearly wanting some sort of heroic insult to be uttered.

I shook my head.

Much actually cursed and glanced at the bishop and knight before darting out into the church yard path. Within seconds, he ducked into the church, wedging himself directly behind me.

"What are you doing?" I growled, sensing the well-wishers in the church were already staring inquisitively at my Merry Man.

"That old, fat, saggy knight is marrying *this* beautiful young bride? Such a waste!" Much shouted in a badly done falsetto tone that was clearly supposed to be my higher-pitched voice.

"That was poorly done Much," I warned, but the bishop fell for it.

"Hold your tongue you cheeky harper," the bishop snarled. "And play your harp."

"That's just it, dear bishop," I said. "I'm hardly a harp player. I always was better at the horn," I said, trying to pluck a few of the harp strings, breaking one in the process. I winced and spun around to shove the harp in Much's hands. "Hang on to that," I whispered.

"What?" the bishop asked, furrowing his bushy eyebrows that nearly became one entity when he glared at me.

"Here, I shall demonstrate," I said before pulling out my white horn. I sounded three, clear blows on it and waited.

In trooped Little John, Will Scarlet, and twenty five Merry Men with Alan-A-Dale and Friar Tuck in their ranks. (Never mind that I had said twenty. Of course Little John had to go and get twenty five.)

"Hello, Father!"

"Morning, Father!"

"Good day, Father!"

My Merry Men greeted the priest as ten of them trooped past the Bishop and the knight and instead hopped into the church, plopping themselves in open pews.

"Fat toad," Friar Tuck insulted the Bishop as he walked up the path and into the church.

"William Scarlet, I may be a bad judge of beauty, but don't these two seem ill matched?" I drawled as I casually strode down the church steps, taking my bow and quiver from Much as he shadowed me.

"They do indeed, Robin Hood. I first thought they were father and daughter," Will Scarlet laughed as he ambled up to meet me, Little John with him.

Will's words caused a stir with the fat knight and Bishop. Instead of continuing to look purple with anger, they turned a distinct green shade of fear.

"And you, Little John. What did you think?" I asked my giant Merry Man.

"I recall a harper lad saying he would gladly wed such a pretty girl. Why, he is here with us. Shall we swap out the groom, Robin Hood?" Little John asked, his eyes mischievously twinkling.

"I think we should. What do you think, Lady Ellen? Would you take our dear Alan-A-Dale?" I asked, stopping in front of the pretty girl, who was practically shaking with fright.

When she heard my words, she visibly brightened. "Alan?" she asked, a smile bubbling to her lips.

"I am here, my love!' Alan said, pushing his way past her parents.

They embraced and cried before Ellen turned away. "Thank you. Thank you Robin Hood, sir," she laughed, wiping tears from the corners of her eyes.

"We shall not stand for this," Ellen's father hissed. "You will not marry that *minstrel*," he spat.

"We will never give you to him," Ellen's mother added in a shrewish voice.

"You won't have to," I gallantly said with my most dashing smile. "I will for you. Lobb, Ryan, please escort this pair away from the ceremony. Much, Will Stutely, and Tom, keep an eye on the knight," I said, laughing from deep in my chest. "Now dear Bishop, please start the ceremony and cry them three times."

"Never," the bishop said, spitting with anger.

"Very well. Then I shall make my own bishop. Little John!" I said.

"Yes Robin?" Little John asked with a wolfish grin.

"How would you like to have a temporary change in careers?"

"Sounds fun. What job shall it be today?"

"Bishop. See if you can fit in our dear bishop's over robes," I challenged.

Little John stripped the outer robes off the bishop with Will Scarlet's help. As the Bishop shouted insults at us Little John poured himself into the robe. The sleeves stopped just past his elbows, and he could not button the top buttons because of his broad shoulders and chest. He could button the ones at his belly, but the bishop was a fat man so it was saggy there where Little John was trim and fit. Finally, the robes stopped just at his knees. He looked like a grown man trying to squeeze into childhood play clothes.

My Merry Men were nearly rolling on the ground. Little John shook his clothes and tried to look ridiculously dignified.

"Cry them, Little John," I said, the only one who did not find the situation immensely funny. I was more worried about being struck dead for such desecration.

"Yes, sir," Little John said with false pride. He cried them, three times, as was tradition. "Announcing the marriage of Alan-A-Dale and… Ellen! Announcing the marriage of Alan-A-Dale and Lady Ellen! Announcing the marriage of Alan-A-Dale and Lady Ellen!" Little John bellowed, flapping his arms in the ill-fitting robe before stopping. "I don't think that was enough," he concluded.

"Really? I think it was plenty," I said. Little John had a **loud** voice, and the church was squat next to Nottinghamshire village. Any patrolling soldiers would be sure to hear him.

"I think I'll do it again. Announcing the glorious marriage of Alan-A-Dale and Lady Ellen! Announcing the divine marriage of the good Alan-A-Dale and the beautiful Lady Ellen!"

"Alright, Little John," I nervously laughed, even as the rest of my men slapped their knees and wiped tears of laughter out of their eyes.

"Announcing the divinely inspired marriage of the good minstrel, Alan-A-Dale, and the beautiful Lady Ellen!"

"They hardly need to be cried six times, Little John," Will Scarlet snickered.

"Announcing the wonderfully divinely inspired marriage of the good minstrel, Alan-A-Dale, and the beautiful Lady Ellen, performed by Friar Tuck!"

"*Thank you*, Little John," I shouted, keeping him from continuing. "I'm sure the rest of the Merry Men in Sherwood heard you. Let's move on."

Some of the Merry Men, headed by Will Stutely once he returned, guarded the fat knight and the Bishop in the churchyard.

Much, Will Scarlet, and Little John, with his Bishop robe starting to rip at the seams, trooped down the aisle.

Deciding to break wedding traditions, Alan-A-Dale and Ellen entered together, with me trailing behind them.

Friar Tuck rattled through the marriage ceremony. I stared straight ahead and paid the event no attention as Little John and Will Scarlet stared at me.

I only spoke up when Friar Tuck asked, "Who gives this fine maid away?"

"I do," I said, a smile curling at my lips. I looked over my shoulder to speak to the guests and the bullied Bishop and knight, who were still being held on the church steps.

They practically shook in their boots.

When the ceremony was over, several of my more exuberant

men yipped and yelled while two others found the church bell tower and started ringing the bells.

"Right, men," I called over the happy shouts of the guests, who threw fistfuls of grain at the newly married couple. "We had better go back to Sherwood. No one, not even the Sheriff, could much mistake the racket we're raising." (Truthfully, I had half expected him or George to burst into the ceremony.)

"Yes, sir!" Little John saluted, the shoulder seam of the robe ripping with the movement.

I blew my horn three times, calling my band to me. "Merry Men, to Sherwood!" I ordered.

"Loved the wedding!"

"Such a pretty bride!"

"Wonderful ceremony!"

My men remarked as they trooped out of the church and started down the church pathway at a jog.

I waved once to Alan-A-Dale and Ellen. They both smiled and blushed as people continued to congratulate them.

I grinned once more in satisfaction, having performed a good deed in spite of my cowardly anxiety, and ran down the path after my men, Will Scarlet and Little John behind me.

We were back in Sherwood in time for a late lunch. Deciding it was too late to travel to Marian's, I stayed in Sherwood Forest and held regular practice with my men before lurking on the road with a party of seven and robbing two squat lords and a murderous, yet equally snotty, squire.

I was just returning to archery practice when one of the men on guard duty came and found me.

"Erm, Robyn, there's a slight problem," my Merry Man started. It was Robert, the ex-tailor.

"Yes, what is it?"

"There is a young man leading a burdened horse and a beautiful maiden through Sherwood. His name is Alan-A-Dale," Robert said.

I frowned. "What's Alan doing in Sherwood?" I muttered, leaving my men behind to train under Friar Tuck's watchful eye.

Robert led me through the forest for ten minutes until we popped out on a small trail. Sure enough, Alan-A-Dale was there with the lovely Ellen and an old horse that had so many saddle bags I suspected Alan and Ellen had packed all of their earthly possessions onto the poor beast's back.

"Alan, what are you doing?" I asked, pushing my way through the bushes, slightly startling the newly wedded pair. (The horse was too tired to notice.)

"Robin Hood! We've come to Sherwood Forest to join your band!" Alan smiled.

"It's Robyn, Alan. R-o-b-y-n. And even though I accept your loyalty, you don't have to live with us," I ruefully smiled. "We are happy enough in Sherwood, but many would not be. Particularly those of the newly married variation," I stressed.

"Alan told me about you, Robyn," Ellen said, alluding to my feminine gender. "We want to be with you. You have no idea what you've done for us. We would like to help."

Alan nodded in agreement.

"Alan can entertain your Merry Men at night, and he is fair with a bow. Surely he could help with hunting. I can take over the darning and sewing, and washing," Ellen continued. Clearly she was the more strategic and grounded of the two.

"Are you sure this is what you really want to do?" I asked. "We'll gladly welcome you, but it *is* an outlaw's life."

Ellen serenely smiled. "If I spent my entire life trying to pay you back, Robyn, I don't think I ever could."

"So let us stay. If we are a burden we will leave," Alan earnestly said.

I laughed. "How could you two be a burden? Very well then, if you wish you can stay with us."

"Excellent!" Much said, crashing out of the underbrush. "I

always wanted to listen to a harper sing tales about your exploits Robyn!"

"I'm sure there aren't any ballads about me, Much," I wryly corrected.

"Of course there are," Little John said, appearing by Much.

"We heard several when we stayed at Nottingham Castle,' Will Scarlet added, popping up at my elbow.

I sighed. I had suspected they were there. Little John and Will Scarlet never were ones to leave me be. "Welcome to Sherwood Forest Alan-A-Dale and Lady Ellen. If you can stand us, then you must have the patience of a saint."

ALAN AND ELLEN'S arrival marked a change for the Merry Men and I. True to her word, Ellen tackled the sewing and washing with a perseverance I envied. Her arrival took a lot of pressure off Robert and me.

Alan raised my already merry band into even higher spirits. Mealtimes became popular entertainment hours. In the evenings, when we usually sat around the campfire and gossiped like ladies in a castle, we listened to ballads sung by Alan, who had the voice of an angel.

In truth, it was Alan and Ellen who inspired the plan I concocted to deal with Marian and her unwanted beau. Actually, perhaps it was not so much inspiration as it was desperation.

Marian did not wait the selected three days for my return. Instead, the morning I was getting ready to go meet her, this time with Will Scarlet and Will Stutely, Tom reported Maid Marian riding through the forest, swearing up a storm with laden saddle bags.

Within minutes, she was in my camp.

"ROBYN!" she bellowed.

"What is it now, Marian?" I asked from my seat by the fire. I was prepared for the fight she was surely bringing me.

"What is it *now*?" Marian hissed, hopping off Nearly Dead. The grey mare sighed and walked herself over to Crafty's pen. "I'm only worrying my head off in my castle tower, thinking about how I'm doomed but my greatest friend is going to help me and solve everything, when lo and behold I hear some village gossip. Apparently Robin Hood is now a *matchmaker*!"

"Marian, they needed help. Ellen was going to be married that day; your father, on the other hand, hasn't even accepted Sir Guy yet," I defended. "Besides, as I reminded you last time we met, you were the one who wanted me to be an outlaw. I'm not your personal hero, Marian. I have other people to think of too."

Marian stared at me and rapidly blinked. For the first time in years, she looked like she was about to cry.

I stammered a little, trying to figure out how to backtrack. The ever eloquent Alan-A-Dale stepped in for me.

"You must be the beautiful Maid Marian," he smiled, running his fingers over his (fixed) harp in a beautiful river of notes. "The apple of Robin Hood's eye, his beloved. Or so the songs say, and they hardly know the half of it. What brings you here, Maid Marian, and so angry? Surely you cannot be mad at your best friend just because she helped my wife and me," Alan gently said.

Marian miserably shook her head and rubbed her eyes with her fists. "I'm coming to stay, Robyn," she whispered. "Father told me in a week he will accept Sir Guy's proposal."

All of the air left my chest and my mind raced. I glanced at Ellen and Alan, Alan's words still dancing around my head. The apple of my eye, huh? I had already stopped one marriage, why not two?

A wolfish smile swept over my lips. "Marian, you and I will return to Huntingdon Castle—"

"Robyn, I—"

"Only to deliver a letter that says you've run off to be with the love of your life, Robin Hood of Sherwood Forest. Write to your Father and tell him that you will have no other man besides Robin, and that he will protect you from Sir Guy of Gisborne. Start writing it," I ordered before turning on my heels. "Alan-A-Dale, I am in need of your help sooner than I thought."

"How can I be of service, Robyn?" Alan asked with a sweeping bow.

"Let us cement the rumor that Maid Marian is Robin Hood's true love," I decided. "Maid Marian may be my best friend, but who says she cannot be Robin Hood's love? It will protect the both of us."

"It's true," Much nodded. "We've been getting lots of women-folk in Sherwood, looking for the bold and brave Robin Hood."

"Marian will be free of the ruse when I dump the Robin Hood mask. It will be perfect," I laughed.

"How can I help you?" Alan inquired.

"Write a ballad. Write several ballads. Make them all about the relationship between Marian and Robin Hood. But it is important, the ballads *must* keep Marian's chastity, as well as my own," I shivered. "I will *not* have bawdy songs being sung about us, nor would I ever want any pathetic lie such as that to be passed around."

"It will work perfectly. You two are already the talk of the town with that sorrowful parting when Robin saved Little John and Will Scarlet," Alan shrugged.

Marian blinked. "My ring got stuck on Robyn's clothes."

"It makes no difference. Once the ballads are out any interaction between you two, no matter how friendly it really is, will be made into the greatest love scene of all time through people's imaginations," Alan said, plucking a few more strings before humming a line.

"What will all of this do, Robyn, except boost your Robin Hood image?" Will Scarlet asked.

"The Sheriff, Sir Guy, perhaps even Prince John, are going to be angry. Very angry. We will draw them here to Sherwood. I will deal with Sir Guy, and we will rob the Sheriff blind," I grinned.

"I like that plan," Little John smirked.

"Me too," Will Scarlet agreed.

Marian only breathed in relief and hugged me. "Thank you, Robyn," she whispered.

Behind us Alan-A-Dale was already singing a few lines.

> *"A bonny fine maid of a noble degree,*
> *With a hey down down a down down*
> *Maid Marian called by name,*
> *Did live in the North, of excellent worth,*
> *For she was a gallant dame."*

7

SIR GUY THE ADDLED

The plan worked perfectly. Almost too perfectly.

Marian, Ellen, and I, all dressed in skirts, swarmed Huntingdon Castle and left the letter on her canopy bed. We also placed a Merry Man in the castle in the guise of a liveryman. He reported on the reactions of Marian's parents and the residents of Huntingdon Castle.

Everyone was scandalized, believing Marian to be the only female in my company of Merry Men. So I had Alan stroll through Nottingham and Huntingdon, singing a made up ballad about Marian's arrival at our camp, which also added that Marian had become fast friends with the other female in Sherwood, Ellen, Alan-A-Dale's wife. (Indeed, the cheeky harper had written a ballad about his wedding, and it was well known already.)

Several days later, my disguised Merry Man reported that Marian's father still feared her reputation was ruined. So I had Alan make the rounds through the surrounding towns again, this time with a ballad in hand that explained that Marian was known as Maid Marian because she and Robin Hood wouldn't marry until Robin Hood was no longer an outlaw and was pardoned and law-abiding.

It worked like a charm.

What I hadn't counted on was all of these surprisingly catchy ballads (Alan-A-Dale is an *excellent* rhymer) enraged Sir Guy, the Sheriff, and even Prince John.

Prince John put a price of 60 marks on my head, which was nothing but a speck compared to King Richard's ransom, but for a man of average wages it was **a lot**.

Whether it was because of the ballads or the price on my head, the Sheriff of Nottingham (or more likely, George) and Sir Guy of Gisborne reacted far faster than any of us predicted they would. Two weeks after we dropped off Marian's letter, they were inside Sherwood Forest without our knowledge.

I hadn't expanded my scouting distance yet because my men and I estimated another few days before the Sheriff would motivate himself to leave the comforts of his castle. Apparently money was a better motivator for the Sheriff than we speculated.

The day started simply enough: breakfast and practice before giving out the daily assignments.

Will Stutely was taking a group of 25 Merry Men with him to canvas the road and look for targets to rob. Much was staying behind to supervise those on guard duty and, surprise, the new trainees that continued to pour into our ranks.

"I think I'll do an outer scouting pass through the forest before I meet up with you, Will Stutely. Robbing sounds like a fair way to pass the day," I yawned before gathering up my bow and quiver.

I *needed* to get out of the camp. Marian had terrorized me during fencing practice that morning. I did not want to be around her gloating face for the entire day.

"Sounds good," Little John agreed.

"Scarlet, are you with us?" I asked, running my fingers over the goose feathered fletching of my arrows.

"No," Will Scarlet said after a moment or two of consideration. "I believe I shall try to rustle up some game. Do any of you Merry Men wish to join me?" he asked.

I blinked and stared as Lobb, Ryan, and two other Merry Men told my usually constant companion that they would join him.

"Will?" I asked, staring at him, drawing his gaze.

He smiled and stepped closer to me to gently ruffle my hair. "It's fine, Robyn. Enjoy your scouting trip."

I was troubled, but Little John was waiting, so I brushed off my green hose before leading the way into the forest.

We talked and walked for twenty minutes, laughing as we swapped lines from Alan's newest ballad, which was about Little John and I and how we met. (Of course Alan didn't say Much had pushed me into fighting Little John, he played it off as my own daring desire.)

"I can't believe he included the part about Will Stutely christening you," I laughed.

"It's a necessary part," Little John insisted. "Most of those who see me laugh on sight about my name unless they are forewarned."

"Well, it was quite funny," I admitted.

"Shhh," Little John said, stopping.

"What?" I whispered.

Little John pointed off to the side and tilted his head. Together we listened to the forest. Someone was walking through our woods.

Little John and I skulked over to the intruder on quiet, sure feet. Little John boosted me up a tree where I spied on the interloper. I nearly fell off the tree due to recoil and disgust when I caught sight of the idiotic fop that had wandered into my forest.

For some reason that I would never be able to fathom, a man had wandered into Sherwood dress in a *horse pelt*. No joke, the skin still had the black mane and tail, which dragged on the ground behind him. The horse's "head" dropped down over the man's skull, perfectly hiding his face.

I slid down the tree and landed next to Little John with a muffled thump.

"Well?" Little John whispered.

"If Crafty was within call I would summon him to kick that intruder's legs until they were broken. The idiot is wandering around in a horse pelt."

Little John winced. The horse pelt thing was a strange case, but it was well known throughout my band that I had finally inherited Marian's love of horses after my adventures with Crafty in Nottingham Castle. The silly wanderer most likely didn't know he was making a somewhat dangerous, if not begrudging, enemy.

"Let's take him out," Little John prompted.

"Are you kidding? I'm not getting any closer to that freak," I hissed.

Little John frowned. "Come on, there is something entirely suspicious about wandering around in a horse pelt."

"No, no I refuse to go near such a barbarian," I stubbornly shook my head.

"Robyn, come on. You're Robin Hood. That whacker is an intruder in *your* forest. You have to go fight him," Little John insisted.

"No, I don't," I hissed. "I'm going to continue with our patrol, looking for the fat Sheriff and George."

"Fine!" Little John said, turning to go back the way we had come from.

"Where are you going?" I hissed after him.

"To find Will Scarlet and go hunting. I can see there's no talking to you whenever it's *that* time for you," Little John said before stamping off.

"It is NOT *that* time for me!" I yowled before turning on my tail and stomping off. Unfortunately my not so hushed fight with

Little John called the horse pelt wearing weirdo right to me. I didn't know it yet, but this mentally disturbed individual was Sir Guy of Gisborne, who was combing the woods in hopes of finding and killing Robin Hood in order to free Maid Marian and claim the reward.

"Hello there," Sir Guy greeted.

I worked hard to keep my features schooled in order to not show my fright or repulse. "Greetings… stranger," I stiffly said. "Can I help you?"

"I am trying to find my way around the woods," Sir Guy confessed in his rumbling voice.

"I know the woods quite well, sir. Is there some way I can assist you?" I asked.

"I am seeking Robin Hood. He has stolen a great prize from me," Sir Guy said.

Instantly it clicked. Only Sir Guy of Gisborne, the broke, cunning, and newly revealed to be incredibly strange, knight would be wandering around Sherwood Forest, alone, looking for me due to recent events. I winced, wondering how Marian would like being referred to as a prize. "It is not wise to seek Robin Hood, sir. Especially in his forest," I honestly said. My Merry Men were only a horn blow away after all, I could have as much false bravado as I wanted.

Sir Guy tilted his head, making one of the horse's ears flick. I wanted to punch him in the face at that exact moment, but Sir Guy continued to speak. "I see you carry a bow. In the spirit of Sherwood would you like to try your hand at a contest?" he asked, holding up his own bow.

I wearily sighed. Were all men, not just my own Merry Men, obsessed with competitions and contests?

"I would rather not," I said, trying to squirm out of it. No use practically *announcing* to Sir Guy who I was.

"Come now," Sir Guy laughed. "What would Robin Hood say if he heard you?"

"He'd agree with me," I muttered, but all the same I strung my bow and tested the string's tightness. "Please go first stranger. What shall our mark be?" I pleasantly asked.

"How about that forked tree?" Sir Guy suggested.

I squinted, looking off through the forest. "That one that was struck by lightning?" I asked. That tree was in my range, just barely though.

"No," Sir Guy said, sounding horrified underneath his horse hood. "The large one, right there," Sir Guy said, motioning to a tree that was probably in the middle of my range.

"Oh, sure. What are we aiming for on it—the seam of the left branch?" I suggested.

"Fine," Sir Guy agreed, nocking his arrow. He released it, and it hit the tree with a thump. It was a decent hit, certainly not the seam of the branch, but it was several hand widths away. "Your turn, green stranger," Sir Guy said.

"Right." I nocked my arrow, moved into the correct stance, and drew with practiced fluidity. I released the arrow, which flew straight and true, hitting the seam of the branch.

"Nicely shot, stranger! Why, you must be as good as Robin Hood," Sir Guy praised.

"Almost," I agreed. No one was as good as my legendary self, not even me. The minstrels and storytellers had blown up my archery talent to be that of a Greek hero's.

"Has Robin Hood recruited you for his band of outlaws?" Sir Guy asked.

"You could say that," I shrugged. There was absolutely no use in lying to Sir Guy. I was going to call my Merry Men to beat him anyway. I needed him defeated in order to return Marian to Huntingdon Castle. And believe me, after enduring her constant presence for two weeks, I was ready to see her leave. If she wasn't rallying my men to perform a stupid deed for me, she was encouraging them to commit insubordination and find helpless tanners, knights, and butchers for me to fight.

"Then let us put aside our bows for a more gallant weapon," Sir Guy decided, tossing his bow aside.

"What?" I stupidly asked.

"Draw your blade... Robin Hood!" Sir Guy shouted before dashing at me, unsheathing his sword.

Thankfully I hadn't yet removed my sword from my side due to fear of Marian randomly popping out and bashing me over the head again. My muscles reacted by pure instinct, and I ripped my sword out of my scabbard, barely lifting it in time to block a blow to my head.

"I knew it had to be you. Only you could wander through the King's forest with such arrogance," Sir Guy triumphantly said.

I snorted. Just yesterday, Much had accused me of slinking through the woods like a kicked dog. My snicker was cut short when Sir Guy leaned down on his blade, increasing the force I was holding back. My arms shook, and I realized I would have to conserve as much energy as possible and blow my horn the second I got the chance. If I was lucky, maybe Little John would return.

Sir Guy drew back for a second to regroup before lunging at me. His blows were easy enough to deflect. The trick was to stay just far enough out of range so I would get the weakest part of the strike.

We continued on this path for ten minutes. Sir Guy viciously attacked, and I defended, never able to release one of my hands from my sword in order to blow my horn.

I was considering dropping the sword and running to climb a tree when Sir Guy paused, panting. "You are fair with the sword," he praised.

I stared at the man as if he were crazed. By this point, Will Scarlet would have thumped me several times for leaving holes in my defense. "Thanks?" I said between taking in gulps of air. I warily slipped my left hand off my sword and felt for my horn.

"Truly, you are a worthy opponent. But I need Marian's

wealth, and I cannot allow you to continue your general disregard for the rules and disloyalty to Prince John," Sir Guy said, taking a step towards me. "I'm going to have to kill you."

I tugged on my horn. Of *course* the straps holding my horn to my belt had to be tangled and twisted, not allowing me to pull the instrument free. "I'm sorry, but I can't allow that," I said, "Not only do I want to live, but I would never allow Marian to be whisked off and married to such an oafish barbarian like you." I pulled harder on my horn.

Sir Guy roared and ran towards me. I took several steps backwards, gliding right under a tree branch. Sir Guy had to hunch down to pass beneath the branch, which gave me the time to side step his thrust. He nearly charged past me, but I pulled my left hand out of the leather horn straps and instead lifted my arm up, clotheslining the knight.

He choked around my arm, but I continued to press, pushing my shoulder into the motion. I managed to throw him backwards. He hit the back of his head on the tree branch he had passed under and fell to the ground with a gurgle.

He landed face down, but I rolled him onto his back after stabbing my sword into the ground. He was senseless. I wasn't completely sure he was unconscious, but he was gasping and his eyes wouldn't focus on me. I plucked his sword from his limp grasp and tossed it away before moving to summon a few men with my horn.

Before I could properly untangle the white horn, Much burst out of a bush right in front of me. "Robyn! Gilbert says the Sheriff and his apprentice are in the forest and heading in the direction Will Scarlet left for, but he couldn't find him—what happened?" Much asked.

"Perfect, your arrival couldn't be timed any better. Do you have any rope?" I asked.

"There's some at a supply nook a few trees back. I'll go get some," Much trailed off before wandering away, casting puzzled glances over his shoulder.

Meanwhile, I tugged the hideously horrible horse pelt off Sir Guy, practically ripping his arms out of the strange sleeves he had fashioned in the hide.

"Who is this?" Much asked when he returned with a length of rope.

"Sir Guy," I grunted, kicking the large man off the horse tail, pulling the entire pelt free of the knight.

"WHO?" Much squeaked.

"Sir Guy. Would you hurry up and help me tie him? He's starting to recover," I hissed.

Much, who was almost as big of a coward as I am, kneeled by my side. "Start with the arms," Much advised before expertly starting to wrap rope around the fallen knight's wrists. "Then wrap rope around his torso so his arms are pinned to his side," Much continued.

Sir Guy made several feeble attempts to wriggle out of the rope, but I kept a foot on his throat, pinning him to the ground in spite of his fussing while Much tied his legs.

"See, now he can't stand without losing his balance and falling over," Much said, straightening up.

"Why are you so good at this?" I nudged a glaring, gagged Sir Guy with the toe of my boot.

"Um, you see, Robyn, the new recruits have to be taught how to escape after being tied up," Much stammered.

"And they can escape this?" I gestured to the trussed up Sir Guy.

"Well, not quite, but, umm."

"Why haven't we taught this art of escaping to our older Merry Men as well?" I asked, tapping my foot on the ground.

"Ah-hah-hah," Much laughed, straightening up while scratching at his head. "So, what are you going to do with him?"

"I'm not sure," I admitted, perfectly aware Much was changing the subject.

"Why don't you cut off his head?" Much suggested.

"Oh gross," I shuddered. My lunch rolled uneasily in my stomach. "No, never. I can skin and gut a deer, but kill an actual human? And by lopping off their head? Ew, no. I think I'm going to be sick." I gripped my stomach.

"Wimp," Much sniffed. "So what do we do with him then?"

"Why don't you figure it out?" I said, walking over to Sir Guy's abandoned horse pelt. I picked it up with a grimace. "I can't believe I'm actually going to put this terrible thing on," I winced.

"What?" Much asked, shuffling to my side.

I shuddered and got goose bumps on my skin in spite of the warm summer air when I slipped my arms into the sleeves.

"*Eww*," Much reacted. "So you'll wear a dead horse but you won't behead a man? Wow, Robyn, you have double standards—"

"Don't talk about it," I begged as the horse's muzzle flopped over my face. "If I think about it I'm going to wretch. Here, take my sword and longbow. I'll have to take Sir Guy's," I said, retrieving Sir Guy's sword. I kept my quiver on my back, hidden beneath the horse pelt.

The knight darkly glared at me and mumbled against his gag, a rag used to clean bows.

"What are you doing?" Much sighed like a worn-out mother as he followed me when I ventured further away to snatch up Sir Guy's bow.

"Disguising myself," I replied, finding an ugly horn that also belonged to Sir Guy. "You said the Sheriff was headed for Will Scarlet, right? I'll draw him away."

Much nodded sagely. "Good plan, just one small problem. *Who is going to draw him away from you?*"

"Release Crafty from his pen. When I blow my horn, he'll come for me. I can ride away and easily lose him in Sherwood," I nonchalantly said, shouldering the quiver. (Really, I was more worried about George than the Sheriff.)

"This is never going to work," Much huffed.

"Then drag Sir Guy back to camp and send some Merry Men after me. I'm not going to chance calling them to my side with the Sheriff about," I said, strapping Sir Guy's sword to my side.

"I just told you Sir Guy can't stand, how on earth am I supposed to transport him back to camp?" Much crossly asked.

"Carry him like a beast of burden. You are an as—"

"Finish that naughty word, Robyn, and I'll string you from the nearest tree by your feet," Much sniffed.

I sighed. "We're wasting time. I've got to run. Thanks, Much!" I called over my shoulder before jogging off through Sherwood, the black horse tail swishing with my movements.

I moved in the direction Will Scarlet had headed for, praying I might be able to catch up with Little John. I did not doubt that Will Scarlet and the slew of Merry Men with him had found the Sheriff. They were most likely hiding and watching the fat, crying aristocrat wander through the forest. I had confidence in my men. We had learned our lesson when we were attacked in winter; none of the Merry Men would repeat that mistake. Panic hadn't yet welled up in me because of that.

At least, I tried to tell myself that I was not frightened beyond all belief as my heart thundered in my throat like a galloping horse.

I reached the peak of a hill and tried to peer through the numerous trunks that blocked my view. There was a tiny meadow at the bottom of the hill. I blinked and squinted at it, but froze when the situation fully dawned on me.

The fat Sheriff was mounted on a chestnut horse, and his men scurried around him like mice or swarming ants. George was there as well. Worse still, Lord Maxine was with him. Both of them were mounted on fine-looking geldings. And worst yet, tied to the trees were Will Scarlet and Little John.

The Sheriff was laughing, and George shouted orders at two soldiers who were standing in front of my men. Under his orders, each one of the soldiers raised a sword to Little John and Will Scarlet's throats.

They swung their arms back, as though preparing to chop their heads off, and I fumbled with the two horns on my belt. I had a choice to make. A very dangerous choice. Call for more Merry Men on my horn and hope it would startle and stop the Sheriff and his men, or blow on Sir Guy's horn and pray it would stop them.

As the soldiers started to swing their blades, I made my choice.

I blew one hard, high note on Sir Guy's ugly brown horn.

The Sheriff turned in his saddle and squinted up at me, spotting me between the forest undergrowth.

I trotted down the hill, my heart pounding as George called for the soldiers to relax. The soldiers in front of Little John and Will Scarlet sheathed their swords and walked back to their formation.

"Hail, Sir Guy," the Sheriff called. "So you found Robin Hood and killed him?"

"Hah-hrum. Oh yes," I said, coughing in my effort to lower my voice. "Robin Hood is dead," I said, stopping next to the Sheriff's tired horse.

"LIAR!" Will Scarlet shouted, thrashing in spite of the ropes that held him against the tree trunk he was tied to.

Little John was ghost-white and looked like his world was crashing in on him. "It's over," he groaned, a noise that started from deep within his soul.

"Did you bring proof?" the Sheriff laughed.

"Yep. His horn," I quickly replied, slipping it out from underneath the horse pelt. I held it up for the Sheriff to see and stifled the burning desire to pull the already drooping horse muzzle lower over my face. I couldn't believe I was *this* close to the Sheriff and he hadn't realized the truth yet!

"You truly are a great knight, even if it *is* in title only," the Sheriff laughed, making his belly jiggle. He slapped his fat thigh when he caught sight of my white horn.

Will Scarlet, on the other hand, burned. "It's a fake! It has to be! She would never let you have it!" he shouted. "*Go to bloody hell!*" he finished, straining against his bonds.

I hoped the Sheriff hadn't heard the 'she' part.

"He's quite upset," I observed, pleasantly surprised that my voice didn't shake like my quaking legs were. It was just as well I was wearing the horse pelt; with it wrapped around me you couldn't see an inch of my shuddering body.

I was frightened out of my mind. If the Sheriff got the merest *glance* at my face…

"Yes. Hearing the death of his master must be quite the blow, even for an aristocratic blackguard like him. The giant seems to be taking it like an abandoned cur," the Sheriff said, his squinty eyes landing on Little John.

"Robyn isn't dead!" Will Scarlet hissed.

The Sheriff rolled his eyes, making George feel that it was necessary to step in.

"For the last time, he is dead!" the young man shouted.

Will Scarlet shook his head and stared at the ground, his eyes not focusing.

"What will you do with them?" I asked.

"Kill them," was the Sheriff's prompt reply. "Now."

"You won't take them back and have them killed before Prince John?" I rumbled.

The Sheriff frowned. "I told you before, if we catch any of those squirming vermin known as the Merry Men, we are to kill them on sight. Holding them will only lure out hordes more, and they'll slip through our fingers."

I frowned and tried to consider the best option that would get me and my men out of the situation, alive. My heart pounded in my throat and I croaked, "Instead of my reward for Robin Hood's head... let me be the one to kill them."

The Sheriff stared down at me as though I had taken leave of my senses. "Are you mad? Robin's death is worth 60 marks!"

"But Robin's death and the death of his two closest comrades, Little John and Will Scarlet, would be quite an accomplishment," I said.

The Sheriff stared at me for several quiet seconds before a fiendish grin settled on his lips. "So you still mean to go after Lady Marian then, even after she's tarnished her reputation by crawling to this wretched forest? Who knows what Robin Hood has done to her—but even so, with her as your bride, you would secure your future livelihood," the Sheriff said, rubbing his chin. "Yes, I'll accept your proposal. I'll take in the 60 marks, and you can claim responsibility for the death of all three men," he laughed.

"Great," I tightly replied, stiffly walking away from the Sheriff. George watched me, his eyes following me as I approached my men.

He was starting to wonder. I could tell by the way he tilted his head and stared at me.

Maxine also stared at me, but with complete disinterest, which I found to be curious. Maxine was not often uninterested.

I pulled the horse hide further around my body and stopped several feet away from my trussed up men. Little John was sagging, and Will Scarlet was swearing like a sailor.

"You two are far too melodramatic," I hissed, soft enough that no one else would hear our interchange as I unsheathed my sword.

Little John froze and stared up at me. Will Scarlet was gap-mouthed for a second before he had the presence of mind to continue swearing, as though nothing had happened.

"Robyn?" Little John quietly ventured, trying to peer beyond my horse hide hood.

"Shhh," I hushed. "George is watching. I'm going to cut you two loose, and then we have to book it. When we get far enough in the woods, I'll call for more Merry Men on my horn. Today's the day we settle the score with the Sheriff," I hissed before drawing back.

"You son of a snake!" Will Scarlet spat at me for effect.

"Draw your last breath, knave!" I shouted, lifting Sir Guy's sword over my head. I swung it down, carefully cutting through Will Scarlet's bindings before repeating the motion with Little John.

The second they were loose, all three of us ducked into Sherwood.

"After them!" George shouted. "That was Robin Hood!"

"Was it?" Maxine asked, sounding politely surprised.

"Go, go, go, GO!" Little John shouted, tearing to the head of our group as soldiers poured into the woods after us.

I nearly tripped and did a face plant when the stupid horse pelt tangled around my legs.

"Robyn, hurry," Will Scarlet hissed as soldiers crashed after us.

"I'm trying! It's this stupid horse hide," I grunted before I accidentally stepped on the black horse tail while running. My knees buckled, and I was on my way down when Will Scarlet scooped me up.

"Hang on," he ordered.

I threw an arm over his shoulders but ripped my white horn off my belt. I leaned against his shoulder and aimed my horn behind Will so I wouldn't blow out his ear drums.

I breathed in before blowing three, quick blasts on my horn.

Within seconds, Ryan and Lobb were with us.

"I sent the other Merry Men back to camp to get help," Ryan said, running alongside Will Scarlet and I. "They should be here soon."

Lobb piped in, "Robyn, what on earth are you wear—" he got out before he was trampled by Crafty, who was bolting for me.

Crafty crow-hopped and narrowly missed kicking Scarlet before he slowed to a prancing trot.

I lunged out of Will Scarlet's arms, shrugging out of the horse pelt before I scrambled onto Crafty's back, working hard to keep from impaling either of us with Sir Guy's weapons.

"Keep going," I ordered, turning Crafty in the direction we were running from before blowing three times on my horn, again.

Ryan retrieved the horse pelt and stopped after Will Scarlet and Little John screeched to synchronized halts. Lobb was twisting over his shoulder to watch me and ran into a tree.

Crafty and I charged ahead. I nocked an arrow on Sir Guy's bow and released it, hitting a pursuing soldier in the shoulder. But he was only one of a dozen foresters that chased after us.

Crafty plunged straight into the swarm of soldiers, scattering them like geese. Behind me, I heard Little John break off branches for himself and Will Scarlet before the duo got to work, bludgeoning soldiers over the head while Ryan calmly shot our enemies with his bow. (Lobb was still stunned and on the ground.)

I took out a second soldier with Sir Guy's bow before Crafty lunged at another man, barely moving in time to avoid an arrow that nearly got me.

Then there was the screeching twang of harp strings breaking. I flattened myself against Crafty's back.

Alan-A-Dale had appeared, ten Merry Men with him. In order to subdue a soldier, Alan had knocked off the man's helmet before slamming his harp down over the man's head. The soldier looked pretty dazed as the harp swung around his neck like a large, wooden collar, the broken strings curling indignantly.

"Alan, what are you doing here?" I barked.

"You called, so of course I had to come!" Alan sweetly said.

I grumbled under my breath before sitting up on Crafty. I brandished Sir Guy's sword over my head, nearly dropping the blasted weapon on my head. "Come on men, let's turn the tide! Capture the Sheriff!" I yelled above the skirmishes.

The Merry Men around me shouted as we overpowered the few remaining soldiers.

As we hurried back to the meadow, more Merry Men, this time led by Will Stutely, gathered at my side. It was everyone Will had taken to set up robberies on the road.

"Sheriff's a bit earlier than expected, eh, Robyn?" Will Stutely laughed in a carefree manner I found very irritating.

I didn't answer and blew my horn three times, yet again, before heeling Crafty.

He was off like an arrow, and we careened into the meadow where the Sheriff waited with no less than thirty five or forty soldiers.

George, Maxine, and the Sheriff stared at me, wondering why I had crashed back to the meadow, seemingly alone.

I tossed Sir Guy's sword away; the blade was practically useless anyway. It was far too heavy for me. Instead I scrambled and nocked another arrow in Sir Guy's brutish bow.

"Give up, Sheriff," I called, training the arrow onto his fat figure.

The Sheriff was white for a brief moment before he remembered all of his soldiers. "Are you *mad*?" he chortled. "You are but one man. *Alone*. No, it is you who should give up," the Sheriff said.

In spite of the Sheriff's confident words, George was gazing around the meadow with shifty eyes, clearly sensing backup was on my trail.

"One last chance, Sheriff. Take your men and return to Nottingham," I ordered. Inwardly, I was cursing my stupidity. I had scrambled out into the open without my men. True, they couldn't be far behind, but it wouldn't take long to make me into a pin cushion.

"Never, you rogue!" the Sheriff proudly snorted.

George glanced at his armed escort and made several covert motions. A row of archers in the back slowly loaded their bows, trailing their arrows onto me.

I swallowed, keeping my arrow on the Sheriff while Crafty snorted and danced sideways beneath me.

My heart thundered in my ears. *What was taking them so long?*

That was when I heard it. The distinct whistle that belonged to Much. He was terribly bad at whistling, so he sounded like a dying sparrow gurgling with salt water. I could recognize that noise anywhere! Several feet behind me in the shadows of the forest, I heard the whine of broken harp strings.

A triumphant smirk crossed my lips. My men had the meadow surrounded. "Very well then," I shrugged. "Have it your way."

"Men!" George shouted, raising an arm to cue his archers.

"*Attack!*" I yelled.

Crafty abruptly burst forward, ducking in front of the cloud of arrows that rained down from the sky.

I released my arrow, which hit the Sheriff's leather hat as a warning mark, knocking it straight off his balding head.

Behind the Sheriff, Much, leading thirty Merry Men, charged out of the tree line. Merry Men poured out of the shadows from every direction. There had to be over a hundred of them!

In the back of my mind, I wondered if anyone had stayed behind to guard the camp.

"Robyn! Your weapons!" Much shouted from across the meadow, brandishing my prized bow in his left hand.

"Coming!" I shouted, heeling Crafty. We plowed straight through the Sheriff's men. There were a few close calls—I was sliced on the thigh with a sword, and Crafty got a wicked looking cut on his rump, but we avoided being shot/impaled by the time we popped out at the other end of the crowd of soldiers.

I threw Sir Guy's bow into the chaotic mess before swooping down to liberate my weapons from Much.

I carefully settled my quiver on my back before I started nocking and releasing arrows in a string of fluid movements.

Down went the man who smashed Will Scarlet in the stomach with a cudgel. Down went the soldier had just opened a wound on Alan-A-Dale's shoulder. Down went the idiot who was strangling a Merry Man against a tree. Down went—

I yipped when Crafty abruptly jostled beneath me and an arrow whistled past me, so close to my nose I swear I could feel the fletching brush my skin.

I twisted and spotted George frowning while nocking another arrow.

Using my legs I guided Crafty in his direction. I did not fix another arrow to my bow. Instead I leaned against Crafty's neck and whacked George in the face with my bow as we passed him.

Crafty spun around, and the whistling twang of another flying arrow told me I had just barely avoided being shot.

Crafty sidled up to George's mount as I reached past the Sheriff's apprentice to grab a fistful of arrows from his quiver. I tossed them out over the ground, significantly decreasing his quiver size.

"Hey!" George cried before swiping at me with a hunting knife.

Crafty danced to the side, and I nearly slipped right off him before straightening up.

I spotted Ryan having some trouble with a soldier, so I quickly plucked an arrow from my quiver, nocked it, and released it. The soldier topped over with a cry, hit in the left shoulder.

Meanwhile, George missed hitting me with another arrow.

My heart stopped for a brief second when I felt the arrow cut through the sleeve of my shirt, but I was also a little stupefied. I was a horse-length away from him, *how could he miss?*

"You really couldn't hit the broad side of a barn could you?" I asked George.

He glared at me, and his horse lunged to the side while he thrust out with his hunting knife.

I adjusted my grip on the bow and held it out, stopping George's blow. (Although the knife made a thin cut in my precious bow.)

George, ever the clever boy, flicked his knife away and instead punched me square in the jaw.

I collapsed on Crafty's neck and toppled over his side. "Sweet saints, what was that for, George!" I irritably snapped, trying to blink stars out of my eyes as I sat up on the ground. "I thought you said you followed the rules you stinking dog turd! That HURT!" I groaned.

"What did you say?" George darkly asked, pressing a sword against my shoulder when I started to stand.

I slowly looked into George's eyes and realized I had made a horrible mistake in my calculations. I had expected George to be as honorable, kind, and chivalrous with Robin Hood as he had been with Lady Mary Gamwell. Obviously, I had thought wrong.

I wasn't a bubbly, mysterious, visiting lady. I was the male outlaw he had spent months hunting, weeks trying to outsmart and out maneuver.

George was out for my blood.

I stared up at George and swallowed, hoping that by some miracle someone would notice my plight.

George smirked and removed the heavy presence of his sword, only to dismount his horse. "You're not what I expected," he informed me, circling me with his sword ready to strike.

"What, not bold and brave enough?" I bitterly asked, turning to keep my back away from him while I looked around the ground. There were a few fallen soldiers; they had to have swords I could borrow.

George laughed unkindly. "Oh no. It is that you are normal. You are cunning and brave, yes. But you are not larger than life. I expected someone more akin to a mythological legend. You, I can beat," he promised, raising his sword.

"We'll see about that," I challenged, throwing myself in a roll. I ducked in time to avoid his blade and popped out of the tumble.

"Robyn," a Merry Man cried, seeing my weaponless state. It was Gilbert. When he got my attention, he tossed me a short sword, a lighter weapon better suited to me.

"Thanks," I called to my ailing man. (Gilbert held his right shoulder, blood dripping between his fingers.)

Concern nagged at me as I hooked my bow over my shoulder, but before tending to Gilbert, I would have to see to George.

I whirled around and brought my sword up in a sad semblance of a defensive position just in time to block George's downward strike.

This did not dissuade George at all. Instead, he fell on me with a flurry of strikes and blows. My body reacted, remembering the seemingly endless morning drills Will Scarlet had trained me through. But in spite of this, I was being pushed back on my heels.

I deflected a blow and took a step backwards before tripping on a dazed soldier Little John had knocked to the ground.

I fell to my rear but managed to raise my sword to block one last blow. George slammed his sword against mine, knocking it out of my grip. It flew through the air and fell, imbedding itself in the ground yards away.

I stared at the weapon with wide eyes before I struggled to ease my bow out from underneath me. I was reaching for an arrow to nock in my bow when George pressed the tip of his sword against my throat.

I froze, scared stiff.

I swallowed, and my heart thumped against my chest when I felt the weapon make a tiny cut in my skin.

"And so you shall fall, Robin Hood. The once Bold and Brave outlaw of Sherwood Forest," George darkly smirked.

He struck like a snake.

One moment the sword was pressed to my neck. The next George was pulling it back to strike me dead, but it never happened.

"*Robyn!*"

There was a sickening crunch when Will Scarlet stepped between George and me. He managed to deflect the worst of the blow with his sword, but George's blade skipped off Will's and sliced his arm.

My world stopped.

"*Will!*" I leapt to my feet.

With grim determination, I lunged around Will. I left my bow behind but instead unsheathed my hunting knife.

"Sorry, George," I whispered in his face. I was mere inches away from him and held my knife to the back of his neck, my arm carelessly tossed over his shoulder while my free hand forced his sword arm down to his side.

George looked shocked—he obviously didn't know I could move that fast. (I didn't know that either, but that is beside the point.)

"I know you're one of the good guys. I really do. But you *have* to stop picking on my men," I told him in a hard voice before spinning my knife and ramming George at the base of his skull with the hilt of my knife.

He went down like a sack of potatoes.

"Will!" I cried, spinning on my heels to clamber to Will Scarlet's side. "Are you feeling faint? We have to get you out of here," I said, placing a hand on his lower back.

Will Scarlet laughed and shook his injured arm. "It's just a shallow cut, Robyn. Hardly anything to be upset about. It only needs a bandage. But never mind me, are you alright?" he asked, extending a hand to cup my cheek.

Air leaked out of me as I leaned into Will. "That was frightening," I whispered, shutting my eyes in spite of the wild pandemonium.

"I know. I came as soon as I could. I was almost too late," Scarlet gulped. "I'm sorry, because of me, you—"

"No, that's not it," I said, pulling back so I could earnestly look at Will Scarlet's face. "I was so scared, I thought he really got you," I said. "I thought… I thought," I stammered, turning bright red.

"You thought?" Will Scarlet said with a roguish grin.

"Never mind," I muttered, avoiding his gaze.

"Is everything OK?" Little John asked, tossing a soldier over his shoulder as he plowed through the fight to reach Scarlet and I. "Did something happen?" he asked, glancing back and forth between us.

"Everything is fine," I said, turning around to plunge back into the thick of things.

"Hold up, we're settling this right now," Will Scarlet said, grabbing me by the scruff of my shirt.

"Settling what?" I grumpily asked as I tried to escape him with no luck.

"Robyn, you need to tell us: are you in love with either of us?" Will Scarlet asked.

Little John blinked, surprised at the sudden question. I squawked. "You cannot be serious, Will. We're in the middle of a fight! This is not the time to talk of love!"

"No, he is right," Little John said, pausing to clobber a soldier in the helmet with his cudgel. "You'll never answer us unless we back you into a corner."

"What happened to waiting?" I protested.

"Robyn," Will Scarlet started.

"It isn't fair," Little John said.

"What?" I asked, wriggling out of Will Scarlet's grip to nock and release and arrow—hitting a soldier that was terrorizing Ryan and Lobb.

"Robyn," Little John said, getting my attention. His eyes were full, serious, and perhaps sad. "I think I know your answer, and it isn't fair of you to keep my hopes up by not responding."

I lowered my bow, feeling guilty and saddened by the brave way Little John straightened up, preparing himself. I shut my eyes—always the coward—but I knew he was right. Little John deserved to know. I had been trying to keep my mind off the Little John and Will Scarlet's confessions, but truthfully the question never should have been asked. I had been in love with Will Scarlet for months, but true to my spineless ways I refused to admit that truth. Even to myself.

I had no doubt that Little John loved me, but to me it was apparent that Will Scarlet's expression of love extended farther. Rather than merely protect me like a guard dog, he endlessly drilled me in the art of swordsmanship to give me the ability to fight back. He was willing to listen to me, and he always found me and searched me out. He was the only Merry Man willing to climb after me when I hiked up a tree.

"It's Will," I finally admitted.

The three of us were still—silent in spite of the chaos that raged around us—until Will Scarlet broke ranks by whipping around to disarm a soldier.

"You're a good man, Little John, and you're as necessary to me as breathing, but Will..." I trailed off, shaking my head.

Little John smiled, his eyes the only hint that my words did injure him. "I understand. I am your right-hand man after all."

I looked away, shamed by the fact that I knew my response had hurt my most trusted Merry Man. Will Scarlet awkwardly rubbed his neck as I stared into the swirling fight, my eyes landing on a flabby backside.

"*Crafty!*" I shouted, spinning around. I flew to my black

horse's side (he was busy ripping apart a soldier's uniform) and threw myself on his back before urging him forward as I checked to make sure my quiver was secure.

Why did I abruptly ride off, leaving my top Merry Men more than a little confused?

Because while avoiding their eyes, I caught a glimpse of the Sheriff fleeing the battle scene, his velvet-clad backside a flaming orange beacon through the green trees.

8

CAPTURING THE SHERRIFF

*C*rafty tore through the battlefield with disregard. With a single glance, I could tell the Merry Men were overpowering the soldiers. Plus with George taken down, there would be no one to give them orders.

"Come on, Crafty," I said, urging the black horse up the hill.

Crafty snorted and threw himself deeper into a gallop as I leaned low over his back. We were gaining on the Sheriff, who was crashing through the woods like a rabid bear.

I narrowed my eyes as Crafty pushed forward. Why did I hear three sets of hoof beats?

My body completely stopped functioning when I noticed that Lord Maxine, on his horse, was riding across from me.

I swallowed and sunk lower on Crafty. No backup would be coming for me this time. I was pursuing the Sheriff too far for my men to catch up to me on foot.

"I'll have to take out Maxine first," I grimly muttered into Crafty's mane. I wouldn't shoot him; there were other ways to trip up a man besides injuring him. Besides, he was still my friend.

I abruptly sat up on Crafty's back and directed my horse over.

We descended on Maxine like ghosts. I tried to shove him out of his saddle before he realized how close we were, but he was too solid.

Maxine swatted me off like I was fly.

I waited a split second, my hand feeling along my thigh. I found my hunting knife, and I pulled it out of its sheath before reaching out and grabbing the rein to Maxine's horse.

My hunting knife was far too dull to ever cut through leather, but Maxine didn't know that.

"Hey!" he shouted, leaning forward to yank my hand off his horse.

Quick as a wink, I tucked my knife up my sleeve and yanked Maxine clear off his horse.

Maxine crashed to the ground with a yelp, and his horse pulled away and slowed down.

I grinned and urged Crafty again. "We've almost got him boy, come on!" I cheered.

The trees were starting to thin. We were almost out of Sherwood Forest.

Crafty and I raced after the Sheriff and his mount.

"We have to make it!" I cried.

The Sheriff was just about to clear Sherwood Forest when Crafty shot forward and turned, streaking in front of the Sheriff's horse. The tired animal reared, dumping the surprised Sheriff on the ground.

Crafty tightly circled the man while I strung an arrow.

"Sheriff," I greeted as the fat man glared up at me. "How kind of you to drop by my forest. But you know, you can never leave Sherwood without first paying your respects to me." I smirked.

The Sheriff's glare disappeared as I anchored my arrow, drawing my bowstring to my chin. Instead, he began to whimper.

"You're in my territory now, Sheriff. You can't cower and hide behind your precious princeling," I hissed.

The Sheriff turned white and started to grovel. "Please, if you release me, I'll do anything! I'll pardon you, I'll tell the Prince you've been killed."

I snorted. "Unlikely. People call you a coward, dear Sheriff, but I know better. I am a coward. You are nothing but a low down *rat*!" I spat.

"Please don't kill me! I beg you!" the Sheriff pleaded, tears starting to spill out of his small eyes.

"I won't, and not out of some favor to you," I told him, cutting off the string of thank-yous he was about to utter. "My men and I don't kill. But we do rob," I leered.

The Sheriff stopped looking so thankful and instead grew nervous.

I was thinking I should perhaps investigate his saddle bags to see why he was so anxious when Will Scarlet charged up, riding George's chestnut horse.

"Robyn!" he cried, relief cracking in his voice when he saw me, my arrow still nocked and trained on the Sheriff. "You're okay," he said, pulling his horse to a skidding halt a few feet away from Crafty and I.

"Yes Will, I'm perfectly—*what are you doing?!*" I shouted when Will slipped off his horse before walking over to Crafty and pulling me off. He hugged me, making me drop my bow and arrow.

"You said it was me, and then you fled. I was afraid you were running off again. What was I supposed to think?" he said. "You didn't give me the proper time to respond!"

"Will, as much as I appreciate the hug you *do* realize the Sheriff could now stab either one of us," I said.

Will, who was facing the Sheriff, reached around my body and elegantly tossed two knives at the Sheriff. One of the weapons hit the Sherriff's cloak, digging it deep into the ground. The other nailed the edge of his tunic into the dirt.

"One move out of him and I'll slit his throat," Will Scarlet said.

Behind me, the Sheriff gurgled.

Will Scarlet leaned his head against mine. "I was afraid you were completely rejecting me."

"What? Where's the sense in that? I *just* told Little John it is you," I said.

Will Scarlet crushed me against his chest for a moment. "I have very little sense when it comes to you. We will talk about this later."

"Oh, certainly. Of course," I agreed, internally planning no such thing. I was going to have to tattle to Much as soon as possible.

The only reason I had confessed at all was because Little John was right. It wasn't fair to him. Just because I knew I loved Scarlet didn't mean anything was ever going to come of it. He was a member of nobility. He was a *lord's son*! I was better off not thinking about it.

Scarlet finally let me go, and I turned so I could properly face the Sherriff.

"So, Robin Hood. What shall we do with this flabby Sheriff?" Will Scarlet said.

"I think we should inspect the saddlebags," I modestly suggested.

"Good idea," Will agreed.

I pulled away from my Merry Man, who cattily smirked at the whimpering Sheriff, and trailed after the Sheriff's horse, which was busy cramming clover in his mouth. (Like animal like owner I guess.)

"Be on the lookout," I called over my shoulder as I opened a saddlebag. "Maxine chased me almost all the way here—by Mary the mother of Jesus," I broke off, awed.

The Sheriff made a whining noise deep in the back of his throat.

"What is it?" Will asked.

"My dear Sheriff," I laughed, hefting my new treasure out of the saddle bag. "What on earth inspired you to bring *this* all the way out *here?*"

Will Scarlet's mouth actually dropped open when he saw what I pulled out of the saddle bag.

It was Prince John's crown.

"You wouldn't be stealing from your prince now, would you?" I snickered, wagging the crown while I strolled towards Will and the Sheriff.

"It was supposed to be bait for you," Maxine called.

I glanced up and in two seconds, I had the crown hanging from my arm, my nocked bow back in my hands. "Careful sir. I don't want to hurt you," I warned my castle friend.

Maxine smiled and slipped off his horse, holding up his arms to show me he was not armed.

The Sheriff was starting to look hopeful, clearly thinking his savior had arrived.

"Sorry, Sheriff, I'm in no position to help. There must be four scores of Merry Men following me," Maxine shook his head.

The Sheriff gasped, surprised at the numbers.

"Only four scores? What happened to the other three?" Will Scarlet muttered.

"Guarding the camp. I hope," I grimly uttered, keeping an arrow trained on Maxine, although I did not pull the string back or anchor it.

"You have seven scores of men? I'm impressed Robin Hood, 140 men is quite a band," Maxine said, slowly edging closer to Will and I.

"140 men," the Sheriff heaved, turning white.

"Don't worry, Sheriff, you'll never see us all at once," I said, uneasy with Maxine's closeness.

I was thankful when Little John, riding one of the horses from the tiny band of mounted soldiers the Sheriff had brought with him, and Marian riding Nearly Dead, burst out of Sherwood.

Right behind them was Much and Gilbert, also riding borrowed horses.

I was relieved to see the extra men, and I'm sure it flashed across my face.

"So this is why you ran off. Is everything alright?" Little John asked, sliding off his horse. He seemed stoic.

"All is well. Where is Sir Guy?" I asked Much, unstringing my arrow, returning it to my quiver. (Maxine would not try to liberate the Sheriff, whom he didn't really like to begin with, in such a crowd of outlaws.)

"Back at camp. I had to drag him the *whole way back*! It took a long time. I left him with Tom and ten other Merry Men. But it doesn't matter, he's out cold," Much shrugged, dismounting his horse.

"How?" I blinked.

"He insulted my chastity, so Ellen slammed him in the head with a stew pot. I hope he wakes up again," Marian considered, innocently batting her blue eyes and winding a piece of blonde hair around a finger.

"That man lost his head. I mean really, insulting Marian and wearing a horse pelt in front of Robyn?" Gilbert grimly shook his head.

I smiled and glanced down at the sweating sheriff. "Much, Gilbert, escort the sheriff back into Sherwood. Strip him before sending him walking back to Nottingham. Leave his horse behind," I ordered.

"Yes sir!" Gilbert smartly saluted, hopping off his horse.

Much rolled his eyes. "Right away," he said in a mock bow.

"Marian, would you go with them?" I asked, rubbing my forehead.

"Why?" Marian demanded.

"Because I need you to decide what we should do with Sir Guy. Plus you need to pack your bags, you'll be returning home soon," I replied.

Marian shrugged and swung Nearly Dead in an arc, moving back to the forest without complaining.

I was both pleasantly surprised and suspicious.

"Come on Sheriff, up you go," Gilbert pleasantly said, hauling the Sheriff to his feet with Much's aid. The two escorted the Sheriff, each clamping down on his shoulder, back to the forest, dragging the horses behind them.

"What are we going to do with this one?" Little John asked, jerking his thumb back at Maxine.

"I'm not sure," I admitted, biting my lip. I could always let him go… "Feel free to leave, Lord Maxine. Someone should notify the Prince that the mission has failed."

Maxine leaned back against his horse. "Check the rest of the Sheriff's saddlebags."

I shot him a cautious look before walking back to the Sheriff's horse, flipping open another saddle bag.

My eyes practically popped out of their sockets. The saddlebags mounded on the backside of the horse were stuffed with gold and jewels, plates, and various regalia.

I quickly crossed myself as I stared at the vast wealth.

"It's part of the collection of the Crown Jewels," Maxine called, still leaning against his horse. Little John was sizing him up while standing in front of me.

Will Scarlet peered into the saddle bags of my shoulder. "For the love of—" he cut off and blinked several times before rubbing his eyes.

I stalked away from the Sheriff's horse and waltzed up to Maxine. "Why does the Sheriff have *the* Crown Jewels?" I hissed.

"He doesn't have all of them. Just a few. Prince John gave them to him. He was supposed to use them to lure you out of Sherwood. Instead, by sheer dumb luck, we stumbled upon Will Scarlet and Little John, who worked as an even better lure," he said, glancing at my Merry Men.

My thoughts raced. The Crown Jewels. *The* Crown Jewels?

"Why does Prince John have the Crown Jewels?" I asked, my mind racing. If I could get them to Queen Eleanor... but no. She wouldn't hawk *the* Crown Jewels just to free King Richard!

"Some of that is inherited from his grandmother. Others are a part of his personal collection," Maxine shrugged. "The Crown Jewels aren't just the crowns the king wears."

Maxine hesitated as Will Scarlet gaped in the saddlebags. Little John didn't move an inch.

"Your orders, Robyn?" Little John asked.

"I don't know. We need Friar Tuck. We'll have to transport them," I said before remembering Maxine was still there and listening. I turned back around to face him. "Maxine, I am not taking you captive. Please return to Nottingham," I stiffly said.

"Robin Hood," Maxine paused. "I'm taking a gamble. I really shouldn't reveal this but... I'm a spy."

In an instant, an arrow was fixed in my bow *again* as I coldly faced Maxine.

"It's not what you think!" Maxine protested. "I'm King Richard's man! I'm one of his spies!"

"Explain," I ordered.

Maxine released a whoosh of air. "When King Richard went on the Third Crusade, he appeared to take his most loyal men with him. However, he knew he had to leave some behind to keep Prince John in line. My family supports King Richard, but none of us could enter the Crusades. My eldest brother is the heir, my second brother had already entered the church, and I was too young to go. Instead, I became a spy for King Richard. I am in contact with those who work to raise the ransom to free King Richard. Rumor has it that you work for that very same goal."

I tilted my head, considering Maxine. It didn't feel like he was lying...

"I have evidence. Written letters from the Queen and letters from knights on the crusades with King Richard," Maxine said before his eyes lit up. "I know a lass who is one of yours. Lady Mary Gamwell, although I'm not sure if that really is her name."

I made a strangled noise in the back of my throat and Little John and Will Scarlet, who had finally finished admiring the jewels, froze.

"Who?"

"Mary Gamwell. She was sought out by your men, Little John and Will Scarlet, directly before they were arrested by George and the Sheriff. I had a bloody hard time getting George off her scent. He was convinced she was their court contact in addition to Lady Marian."

This made Will Scarlet laugh.

Little John wasn't long behind him.

"Shut up!" I hissed, although I was relieved to hear Little John laughing.

"You *really* must have done a stellar acting job," Little John said, slapping his knees.

I raised my eyes to the sky. "Thank you for practically *giving* my identity away in front of a stranger."

"He's no stranger, he's King Richard's man," Little John hummed.

"Plus you got along with him *oh so well* at that masquerade party," Will Scarlet sniped.

"Wait... what?" Maxine asked, his eyes traveling back and forth between my men and I.

"ENOUGH!" I bellowed, silencing Little John and Will Scarlet. I turned to Maxine, clearing my throat. "Maxine, if you can indeed procure evidence that you are one of King Richard's men, and you can be in contact with the Queen, my men and I will do everything we can to aid you."

"He's one of the King's, alright," a voice called out from Sherwood.

I glanced up to see Friar Tuck waddling out of Sherwood Forest, panting and turning red.

"Whenever you cause a stir, you have to situate yourself as far away from me as possible, don't you?" the Friar complained, stopping to breath.

"Hello, Friar Tuck, are you a soothsayer?" I teased.

"No," Friar Tuck grunted. "Or I would have seen you coming *miles* away at that river. I heard you blow your horn and went to investigate it. By the time I arrived, I was told you went chasing after the Sheriff with some of your best men. I ran into Much and Gilbert on the way back; they told me to continue on," Friar Tuck shrugged.

"I'm glad you found us," I smiled.

"What did you say about Lord Maxine?" Will Scarlet asked, glancing at Maxine.

"I put the word out among the church and received several confirmations. Queen Eleanor is confiscating some of the gold and silver church artifacts and is hawking them for King Richard's ransom. Additionally, land taxes were raised," Friar Tuck said.

"But what about Lord Maxine?" Will Scarlet repeated.

"Patience, man, I'm getting there!" the Friar huffed. "A friar in Yorkshire confirmed my suspicions. King Richard has men spread through England who act as his spies. Maxine is one of several who shadow Prince John and follow his movements."

"How do you know that?!" Maxine yowled, startled.

"You underestimate the power of the church, my boy," Friar Tuck chided. "It was two abbots who discovered King Richard's location in the first place."

"Lord Maxine, how far down the chain are you from Queen Eleanor?" I asked.

"Not very far. I could easily ride to her court if I had to. Why?"

"My men and I have raised a decent chunk for the ransom. If you could deliver it to Queen Eleanor, along with Prince John's ridiculous bait, I would be in your debt," I said.

"Of course, I would be glad to help in any way I can. Although I might need a day before I leave Nottingham. How much have you gathered?" Maxine asked.

"I believe we're up to approximately 34,000 marks. Not including the treasure in these saddlebags," I said, glancing at Little John and Will Scarlet to confirm my guesses.

"That sounds about right," Little John agreed.

"Knights have been lured to the forest by promises of a reward from Marian's father. It's been a busy two weeks," Will Scarlet acknowledged.

"34,000 marks?" Maxine uttered, his mouth hanging open.

"Yes, I know. It's only a fraction of the ransom," I sighed.

Maxine laughed. "It is a tidy sum. You have no idea how much it will be appreciated. I will ride to Queen Eleanor as soon as possible."

"That's no good," Will Scarlet flatly rejected. "If you ride off alone, it's practically announcing you're linked with us or King Richard."

"What do you mean?" Maxine asked, bewildered.

Little John rolled his eyes. "It's fairly obvious. If you leave our forest, unharmed, that apprentice fellow of the Sheriff's will be immensely suspicious of you. Especially when the Sheriff reports you told us Prince John's crown was bait for us."

"It will be even worse when you prance in, unhurt, while the Sheriff goes in his underclothes, and George and the rest are injured and bruised. I could have some men drop you off at the gates, but I'm not willing to go any farther than that to make the façade complete," I warned. "No, we'll have to give you a *reason* to go."

"Send Marian," Friar Tuck shrugged. "She was at Queen Eleanor's a year ago. It is not preposterous that her father would whisk her off to that location once she returns home."

I stared at the portly churchman. "How did you know that Marian stayed in Queen Eleanor's court?"

"It's common knowledge," Friar Tuck said, waving it off.

"No, it's not. I didn't know that," Little John said.

"It's a good idea. If Marian tells her father she wants to go to Queen Eleanor's courts, he'll cry with joy, and of *course* she'll need a male escort with some courtly standing in addition to all of her maids," I said, rubbing my chin. "And we can always spread the rumor that Lord Maxine was blackmailed by Robin Hood into journeying with her, and that was his price to return safely to Nottingham without us seriously harming him," I decided.

"If we snag a few pieces of his clothes and rough him up a little, it will work perfectly," Little John agreed.

"Let's do it," I decided. "If you're willing, Lord Maxine."

"I am. But will Marian be?" Maxine asked.

I snorted. "If we tell her she's accompanying our monetary donation, she'll be more than willing. She'll be demanding," I laughed, walking past Maxine to collect Crafty. "Please return with us to our camp in Sherwood, and we'll start planning, Lord Maxine," I invited, swinging up onto my wicked horse.

Lord Maxine was staring at me as though he were seeing me for the first time. "…Lady Mary?" he asked.

I gripped Crafty too tightly with my legs, so he threw his head and hopped in protest.

"You didn't get Will and Little John's obvious hints, but when you see me on a horse you instantly recognize me?" I sighed.

"That's Nightmare, Lady Mary's horse. He wouldn't let anyone touch him except for her. Plus you do sound a lot like her," he said, squinting up at me through narrowed eyes. "So Robin Hood's a girl?"

"Um, no. I was just disguised as a girl," I simpered, trying to cover my tracks.

"You forget, Robin… or Mary. I danced with you. I *know* you're a girl," Maxine said, shaking his head.

I groaned and stared up at the sky as Crafty fidgeted. "Will all of Britain know I'm female before this century is over?"

"Quite possibly, but I doubt it," Little John said.

"Who would want to admit they've been robbed by a girl?" Will Scarlet agreed.

"WILL, LITTLE JOHN! NOT HELPING!" I shouted.

"She's like this a lot," Little John whispered to Maxine.

"You better not tell the King. She'll be so disappointed," Will Scarlet added.

"YOU TWO!"

"Sorry!"

I glared at Scarlet, giving him the evil eye, before looking to Little John. He had a rueful smile on his lips, but he nodded.

It would take some time…but we were going to be fine.

TRUE TO HIS WORD, Maxine escorted a very torn Marian to Eleanor's courts. (She was beyond ecstatic to be doing some of the actual outlaw work, but she was chagrined about returning to Eleanor's ladies.)

Throughout the months, Friar Tuck kept us updated on the ransom status. Queen Eleanor did hawk some of the Crown Jewels and pawned many church treasures.

We outlaws continued to rob all through the rest of fall and into the winter when the ransom money was finally sent. In the end, only a little over 100,000 marks were sent to Henry IV of the Holy Roman Empire. He took the price and freed King Richard, even though it wasn't the full ransom. King Richard was officially freed February 4, 1194.

He returned to England by March, and the second week into the month, my Merry Men and I found a royal parade at our doorstop.

9

KINDLY MONKS

"Does he really think we're actually going to rob him?" I asked Maxine as I stood on the branch of a tree, watching King Richard and his men parade through Sherwood. Again.

"I think he's hoping you'll at least pop out so he can say hello," Maxine groaned, clinging to the tree trunk with the death grip of a man not used to such heights. (This was why I was usually the only one to climb high in the trees.)

"You think he would figure it out after we didn't touch him those first few days," I said, watching King Richard ride underneath me on his beautiful white stallion. Again.

The first time the King came through my men and I bowed at him from the shadows, unseen by the monarch and his company. The second time he came through, we continued to watch in awe. Same with the third, fourth, and fifth time.

It was now the eleventh ride, and I was starting to grow impatient.

With the King parading up and down the road through Sherwood, greedy merchants and aristocrats would join with him, since the news was spread far and wide that my men and I had not moved to rob him.

"Tell him we won't reveal ourselves. Not ever!" I emphasized.

"I would, but then he would know I'm in contact with you and would most likely order me to lead him to you," Maxine said, glancing down at the glittering procession before grimacing, "Do you always have to climb this high?"

"He can't have come all of this way just to see my Merry Men and me," I scoffed. "Surely the King has more important things to be doing."

"True. His original purpose in coming to Nottingham was to force his brother to heel. It was a well-known fact that Prince John's been holed up in Nottingham for months. King Richard came to confront him."

I snorted. "Confront? Queen Eleanor, ever the mommy, made both King Richard and Prince John apologize to each other and said they were bad children."

My usual awe and wonder at royalty was wearing off. *Fast.* King Richard would cripple my outlaw practices at this rate. Besides, hearing royal trumpets for eleven days straight was enough to make anyone testy.

"It didn't quite happen like that. King Richard, thanks to Queen Eleanor's gentle encouragement, kindly said his brother was misled and improperly incited to rebel," Maxine corrected, a thin sheen of sweat covering his forehead. "Can we climb down yet?"

"Go ahead. I'm going to signal my men to start laying pebbles down again. If we're lucky, a horse will get one wedged in its shoe, and they'll have to return to their court," I said, leaning off my branch.

There was a thump and the rustle of leaves. I straightened up and blinked once before smiling Will Scarlet appeared, scaling the trunk of the tree. It took him some fancy maneuvering, but he made it to the branch over my head. I peered down at the ground, and, sure enough, Little John was at the base of the tree trunk, looking up at me.

They never liked leaving me alone with Maxine. (Will Scarlet especially.)

I fixed my balance and peered up at Will again. "Hello, Will. We were just about to come down. I need to tell Tom to begin spreading the pebbles." I gripped onto the tree trunk and started to slide down. "Help Maxine down, please?

"Too late, I'm already following you," Will said, hopping from branch to branch like a cat.

"Will, you can't just leave Maxine up there. WILL!"

Once safely down the tree, Maxine said his goodbyes.

"Please, somehow, tell King Richard. Or allude that Robin Hood and his band of Merry Men will never, *ever*, ever stop him on the road," I instructed.

"Right," Maxine said, weakly throwing an arm in the air before stomping off through the forest.

"Little John, signal down the line that we need to throw the pebbles to hopefully make a horse temporarily lame. Tom should be in position," I said, turning to my second-in-command. "Scarlet and I will head back to camp."

"Oh yes, Marian managed to sneak into Sherwood. She's chatting with Ellen at the moment, but having King Richard around is making her angrier than a mad hornet. Her mother is positively *wild* with glee because of all the knights King Richard's toting with him," Will Scarlet laughed, slipping an arm around my shoulders.

"Oh that's fantastic," I muttered, shrugging the arm off me. I was still avoiding the topic of love like a leper, and I had set both Much and Will Stutely on Will Scarlet, but he was still being a blockhead and refused to be dissuaded from me. (That still didn't change the fact that he was a *lord's son*!)

"Plus, there's a new recruit who needs to be christened and sworn in. We also have the requests from Nottinghamshire;

apparently taxes are going up again, even with King Richard's return. We need to decide how to start spreading the money," Will Scarlet continued as we started walking through the forest.

"And what of George? Has he been sending any more foresters to poke around Sherwood? Those last two nearly made it past the scouts," I said.

"He's been quiet. He'll probably start moving against us when King Richard grows bored with Sherwood and leaves," Scarlet replied.

"One of our men in the Nottingham kitchens said George is still brooding about Robin Hood's real identity. He might be on to you, Robyn," Little John added, trotting after us, having made the signal.

"Wonderful. Well, if we can't rob, at least George can't move to get us," I concluded.

"Isn't that the truth."

"All the same, I'll be looking forward to the day King Richard leaves."

"Will! That's a terrible thing to say! I'm ashamed to call you one of my best men!"

"I'm just saying what you're thinking."

"You *rude, inconsiderate* creature! I love my King!"

"Oh sure you do. Until his trumpets start ringing in your forest *forever*."

"For the love of all that is still pure in this unholy world, I hope not."

THE FOLLOWING MORNING, I was *sprinting* down the road that twisted through edges of Sherwood Forest.

Why, you ask, was I running?

Because Little John, Will Scarlet, Much, and Will Stutely were in hot pursuit. Apparently, they found a rogue knight, a rogue *knight*, passing through the forest early that morning, and they wanted me to fight him. *Me*, quite possibly the weakest member in our band.

I did not take to that idea kindly, so I was forced to run away. Unfortunately, my Merry, and insane, Men followed.

I managed to ditch them sometime between releasing Crafty upon them and jumping across the river.

"Head to Nottinghamshire. It's the safest place," I told myself as I jogged along. "I'll hide with Much's parents. No one will look for me there," I muttered as I booked it around a turn in the road.

I was moving so fast and I wasn't prepared to find another person on the road, so I smashed straight into a brown-robed abbot. I bounced right off the fellow and landed on the ground with a smack.

In an instant, I was up. "Sorry, sorry, so sorry. I didn't hurt you did I? No? Good. So sorry, I must run." Every particle of my being howled that I had to get going *now*.

If my men were to see me with the abbot, they might make me fight him just to satisfy their twisted sense of honor.

As I righted myself, I took notice that I had run into a veritable *pack* of abbots. There was not one monk but *twelve*.

"Making a pilgrimage?" I politely asked, pausing.

"One could say that. Yes," said the abbot I had rammed into, his hood pulled low over his face. His voice was melodic and surprisingly deep.

"Ah, good luck," I said as the other monks twittered around the abbot, patting him off. "Good day," I called before I was off like a shot.

Some distance down the road, I stopped and turned around to observe the monks again.

They were churchmen. Men of *God*. And oddly none of them sported the sagging belly that Friar Tuck and his compatriots seemed to have.

"They're going to get trampled by King Richard and his

procession," I muttered. "But if I stick around the chances of the others catching up to me drastically increase." I groaned and rubbed the sides of my head, "*Curses!*"

That drew the attention of the twelve abbots.

"Sorry!" I chorused, quickly crossing myself before bolting back to the front of their group. "Dear men, are you not well? I cannot help but notice your lack of… of… girth," I said making an imaginary pot belly with my arms to illustrate my point.

The head abbot tilted his head. "Excuse me?"

"You aren't fat. Are you fasting? Or has your pilgrimage really been that difficult?" I inquired.

"We have come far," one monk piped in.

"Not *that* far," the head abbot corrected.

I weighed out my conscience and sense of survival.

I try to do good things for people whenever I can. At this point, I was still a little terrified that I would be sent to hell for my pleasant life of banditry. This was the perfect time for me to do something good, especially for a man of God. (I imagine I hadn't won any points with my mistreatment of the bishop at Alan-A-Dale's wedding.)

… But when my Merry Men caught me back at camp I would *have* to fight that knight!

I mulled over it before deciding. "Men, how would you feel about dining with me and my company?" I exhaled, yanking the invitation out of me.

"Who are you?" the abbot I had smashed into asked. Apparently, he was their spokesperson.

"I am but a humble forester. I, however, know it is wise to treat a man of God kindly," I groveled and scraped.

"The only one who lives in this forest is Robin Hood and his band of outlaws," the head abbot laughed.

"Robin Hood and his band of Merry Men," I automatically corrected. Alan-A-Dale said calling us outlaws was bad for our reputation. Friar Tuck laughed him out of the camp after that proclamation. "Yes, they do live here too… unfortunately," I growled.

"Do you know him?" the head abbot asked.

"Who?" I hooted, blinking quickly.

"Robin Hood. Looking at your clothes I had initially assumed you might be one of his bandits," the abbot said, motioning to my lincoln green getup.

When picturing Robin Hood, people were *always* looking for someone with broader shoulders and a more muscular build. Someone like Will Scarlet.

"Aherm," I said, avoiding the abbot's hooded gaze. "Well… I—"

"*Robyn!*" Little John bellowed like an ox.

"Stop right there!" Will Scarlet shouted after him.

I inquisitively turned around and yelped when I saw Will Scarlet and Little John racing towards me. There were two distant specks further down the road. Much and Will Stutely probably—they never had very good running stamina.

"Sorry, I must go," I said, bowing out of the abbots' company.

"Do not dare, Robyn!" Will Scarlet shouted. They were gaining on me.

I zipped through the monks, spying freedom further down the road. "Almost, there," I grunted, pushing past the last monk. I made a flying leap, and Little John fair snatched me out of the air.

"Oh no, you don't." He yanked me backwards.

I slipped out of his grip and headed for a tree. I threw myself on the lowest branch of a thick oak when Will Scarlet caught me.

"Give it up, Robyn, I've got you," he grunted. "Ow, stop kicking!"

"No! Let me go! I don't want to fight that knight! He'll *kill* me!" I said, halfway to hysterics.

"Marian said she thought you could take him," Little John piped in, watching me kick Will Scarlet in the chest.

"That means nothing. I could probably beat him in archery, but of course, the men I fight *always* get upset whenever I beat them and turn on me with a sword!" I said, pausing before furiously kicking some more. "Let me *go*, Will Scarlet, or I swear I'll hide your favorite sword!"

"No. Get. Down!" Will Scarlet said before latching his arms tight around my waist and picking his legs off the ground.

We dangled in the air for several seconds before the branch snapped and we tumbled to the ground.

"I won't do it! You can't make me!" I said, my voice edging into a wail.

"Yeah, right," Will Scarlet grunted, sitting up off the ground.

"I can't do it! I'm… busy!"

"With what?" Little John asked, latching a hand around my wrist before he pulled me up into a standing position.

"These monks. I have offered them the hospitality of Sherwood Forest!" I gallantly beamed, spreading my legs and planting my fists on my sides in a reasonable impression of my dashing and bold Robin Hood persona.

"…So *you* are Robin Hood," the head abbot said after staring at me for a while.

"Sorry to disappoint you," I snapped, hearing the distinct frown in his voice.

Will Scarlet smacked me upside the head. "That is *not* the way to talk to an abbot."

I frowned and smashed my elbow into his abdomen. He went down with a gurgle.

"Bloody hell!" Will groaned.

"You shouldn't swear in front of abbots either!" I pointed out.

"See, that was cheating. You hurt him *before* he swore," Little John calmly coached.

By this time, Will Stutely and Much had stumbled far enough down the road to catch up.

"Robyn, no good," Much panted.

"Knight, left," Will Stutely heaved.

"Really? What happened?" I asked, straightening up.

"Marian," Much wheezed.

"Oh. Well, all is well that ends well," I said, yanking my hand out of Little John's grip. "Dear abbots, allow me to introduce myself," I said, taking several steps away from my men before fixing my dashing smile on my lips. Gone was the whiny, cowardly Robyn. "I am Robin Hood, and welcome to Sherwood Forest, my humble abode," I said with a flashy bow I learned from watching George at Nottingham castle. "These are some of my Merry Men. This giant here is Little John, my second-in-command," I said, pointing to Little John as Will Scarlet walked up to me and tossed an arm over my shoulder.

Little John nodded at the abbots and rested his cudgel on his shoulder.

"Over there is Much and Will Stutely, my childhood friends and first and second Merry Men."

"Greetings," Much breathed, finally able to stand upright.

"Why do we always have to be introduced together in a single sentence?" Will Stutely complained.

"And this man," I said, indicating to Will Scarlet, who still had his arm on my shoulder. "Is Will Scarlet, my…second-second-in-command?" I wondered. I was always hesitant when introducing Will Scarlet. I didn't really know how to describe his place in the band.

"Almost," Will Scarlet said, winking at the abbots. "More like this," he said before kissing my cheek.

"Would you get *off* me?" I said, pushing him away before scrubbing at my cheek with the back of my right hand, giving Scarlet a withering glare.

I turned back to the monks and pleasantly smiled. "Men, it would bring me great pleasure if you would dine with us for lunch. The good Friar Tuck will be there. I am sure he would enjoy speaking to you about… Godly things," I said, flourishing with my hand.

The abbots were quiet for a moment. "It would be our honor," the head monk decided.

"Excellent. One moment please," I said, clapping my hands before turning to my men. "Did Crafty happen to follow you?"

"No. Thankfully," Much glared at a hole in his green tunic—likely one Crafty had made.

"Why?" Will Stutely asked.

"I don't want to have to track him through the forest for the whole day again," I sighed before bringing my horn to my lips. I blew three times before returning it to my side. "I'll dispatch two men to herd him back to camp."

"Excellent plan," Will Stutely piped in. "I'm very grateful you aren't sending us after him."

"I have worse things planned for you," I said before turning to the monks. "You'll have to give me a minute or two. There are tasks and missions that must be given out. As soon as my men arrive and I break down the day, we will be free to return to camp."

"Do all of your men come to your horn?" a monk inquired.

"No. That would bring about utter chaos," I laughed in the manliest voice I could muster.

"We rotate duties," Much told the monks. "Every day, the men are divided up. Some are assigned guard duties, others go to the road for... uh... robbing, and many stay behind in the morning to train, hunt, and maintain our camp grounds. Every day a group of Merry Men are assigned to come to Robyn's call on the horn. Unless he blows three times, and then three times again sometime later. Then we all come as quickly as possible," he finished.

"And here they are," I said as twenty-five Merry Men popped out of the forest, wanting to know what was wrong.

"Are these blackguard abbots, Robyn?" Lobb shouted.

"Shut your trap and listen," Ryan hissed.

"Robyn's about to speak. SHHH," Gilbert announced.

"Men, these abbots will be enjoying our protection and hospitality for the morning. Remember that," I shouted. My Merry Men hushed themselves and listened to me. "They will be eating lunch with us and perhaps enjoy a ballad or two sung by Alan-A-Dale. But before we dine, there are several tasks that need to be completed. Ryan, take Lobb and Gilbert and sweep the road. Make sure it's ready for King Richard, bless his soul, and his wretched procession. Most importantly, *be sure to get rid of the pebbles from yesterday*. That was very fortunate that King Richard's horse got the pebble rammed in his hoof, but we'll wait to see if it's necessary to throw more today if they keep up that incessant trumpeting."

"Right, Robyn!" Ryan bowed before motioning to Lobb and Gilbert. The three were gone in a flash.

"Rob, I'm sorry, but I need you and David to go get Crafty. You can take a dried apple or two from his barrel. That should put him in better spirits," I continued.

"Yes, Robyn." Rob winced before disappearing with another Merry Man, David.

"Hob, Tom. I know I already sent out a hunting group this morning, but I did not expect to feed a herd of monks. I need you to go out and bag some more game," I said, slowly ticking down my mental list of chores.

"You got it," Hob winked before heading to the woods with Tom.

"Don't be excessive!" I called after them before turning my attention onto another Merry Man. "Fisk, please run ahead to camp and let everyone know what is going on. I don't want to enter the camp and find Marian prancing around, brandishing a sword over her head, *again*."

"Yes, sir!" Fisk, a very eager trainee, saluted before taking off, running through the forest.

"If a group of you could watch the road and keep an eye on King Richard, that would be excellent. I don't want a repeat of that time his procession nearly ran into that traitorous snake of a lord that lives in Prince John's pocket. We *cannot* have an assassination attempt on our King in our forest. That is all, thank you," I said before turning to the abbots. "Please, our camp is this way," I said before leading the way into the forest, Little John and Will Scarlet walking on either side of me.

As I led us through the trees, Merry Man flashing in and out of view as they followed the monks and I, I heard the head abbot mutter, "His men are more at his bidding than mine are at mine."

We reached the camp after half an hour to an hour of walking. (They may be monks, but I am not stupid. I would never lead a stranger to my camp without taking a winding, confusing, impossible-to-trace path there.)

"Hail, Robin Hood!" several of my men shouted when we entered the camp, the sign with the golden arrow hanging over the top signaling we were home.

I grinned and called them by name before shaking them off as we pressed further into my abode.

"Do you know the names of all of your men?" an abbot asked.

"Names, their life story, their families too, if they're from the area," Little John answered for me.

Alan-A-Dale greeted us, already plucking a few notes on his harp. "And here comes Bold and Brave Robin Hood," he smiled.

"Hello, Alan. Where are Ellen and Marian?" I asked the minstrel.

"I'm not sure. Last I saw them, they were helping Rob coax Crafty into his pen. Friar Tuck is working on a fine fish stew though, and Ellen was roasting deer meat before Crafty arrived. Even better, three Merry Men came back with four bucket loads of berries. We'll have an outstanding lunch today," Alan smiled.

"Excellent," I smiled.

"Let's eat!" Little John enthusiastically bellowed.

Lunch was a fine affair, as usual. The camp was filled with laughter as my men re-told some severely revised stories about me. The ballad in which Little John and I met was a great favorite, as was the one that dove into the complex 'relationship' between Marian and I.

(To assist us in deceiving the monks, Marian sat next to me during the dinner, laughing and behaving beautifully while occasionally fawning over me.)

"Alan, tell the story about your wedding again," Lobb called. "I love picturing Little John in that ridiculously small bishop robe."

"What of the ballad of Sir Guy of Gisborne," an abbot called out. "Is that not popular?"

"It is, only because so many of Nottinghamshire's peasants love bloody stories," I sighed. "It wasn't really that gruesome, all things considered."

"You mean to tell me you didn't cut off Sir Guy's head?" the head abbot inquired.

"No," I laughed. "That was Alan, speaking symbolically. We figure Sir Guy must have lost his head to tramp around my forest in a horse pelt. No, we actually dumped him off at a monastery in the north. I'm not sure what he's up to nowadays."

"What about the fight with the sheriff?" some men asked.

I winced. "That was a little bloodier," I consented. "I didn't lose any men, but some were badly hurt," I said, my sad eyes turning to Gilbert.

"I'm fine now," he huffed from his log across the camp.

"I know," I shrugged, aware that the atmosphere of the camp was now quite dreary. I abruptly stood up, upsetting Marian and Little John, who were next to me. "Well men, we've had a good meal and Alan-A-Dale has entertained us all enough. Now it's our turn to play. Dear monks, would you like to observe our romping practice?" I asked. I always hated it when I had to talk like the perceived version of Robin Hood. I sounded like a blithering idiot. I mean really, romping practice?

The abbots ate it up, like everyone else. "How do you practice?" the head abbot asked.

"Through competitions of a sort," I said, motioning for my

men to clear the camp and set up for practice. "For archery, there is a target you *must* hit."

"And if you miss it?" a monk inquired.

"Then you get smashed on the head by the good Friar Tuck," Little John wearily said, having been the recipient of many head smashes.

"I don't practice. Strictly speaking, I'm not a Merry Man, so I'm an impartial judge," Friar Tuck laughed.

"We also have cudgel practice and swordsmanship for a group of us, as well. With those sports, you get your smacks naturally when you mess up," I said, taking my bow from Marian, who fussed with my clothes for appearance's sake.

"Robyn always does the best in archery," she proudly smiled, as though she owned my talent.

"Yes, but even I was punished once," I cringed, recalling the moment. Instead of smashing me on the head, the good Friar tucked me under his arm and dragged me about like I was a child for an hour. It was a humiliating experience. I would have preferred the smack in the head.

"The archery range is ready," Gilbert announced as a Merry Man tied a rope to the target and secured it to the tree. The target dangled from the branch, swinging in the breeze.

"Won't that make it harder?" a monk asked.

"Exactly. We don't hit stationary targets very often," I said, stretching my limbs. "Who is up first?"

One by one, my men paraded through the range, many hitting it, a few missing it. Those that did miss bore Friar Tuck's blows with good cheer.

Finally, Will Scarlet was up. "Allow me to show you, good monks, how a real archer shoots," he boasted.

Some of the Merry Men jeered and called him out.

"Boaster!"

"That's puffed pride you've got there, Scarlet!"

"Robyn will tan your hide!"

Will Scarlet ignored them and nocked an arrow before lifting the bow up. He pulled back, anchoring the arrow by his chin, and aimed.

Just as he was about to release his arrow, Marian, ever the sneaky girl, spoke. "Will Scarlet is called Scarlet because he blushes red whenever Robyn looks at him," she announced.

Will wobbled as he released his arrow. The shot was off. *Way* off. It actually hit the trunk of a neighboring tree rather than the dangling target. Will spun on his heels. "Marian," he hissed.

The rest of the Merry Men snickered.

"She got you good!"

"Down with the boaster!"

"Has he turned scarlet yet?"

Although Will Scarlet still professed to be profoundly in love with me, he wanted to be the improper peter who brought it up. He greatly disliked others singing about it—I suspect because he thought I would change my mind about him.

Marian smiled sweetly.

"That was hardly fair," Will Scarlet declared.

"Take your blow from Friar Tuck, Scarlet, and man up," Little John chuckled as he checked his bow before striding up to the firing point.

Will Scarlet grumbled. "You'll get yours, Little John," he noted, dutifully walking over to Friar Tuck.

"He will be punished even though it was all in jest?" the head abbot asked, coming to stand next to me.

"Of course. We all play such tricks on each other, but if we're actually in a heist, we cannot afford to react to such insults," I explained. "If we are off target by even a little, we might accidentally kill someone," I said.

"Sorry, Scarlet. Rules are rules," Friar Tuck chuckled before smashing Will Scarlet in the head, sending him tumbling to the ground.

"Come on, Little John," Much called, ignoring the scene. "My granny can shoot an arrow faster than you."

"Prince *John* could shoot an arrow faster than you," Will Stutely cackled.

"Men, behave yourselves," I lectured.

"Yes, Robyn."

Little John breathed deeply, nocked the arrow, took the proper stance, and anchored his hand.

Milliseconds before release, Marian again opened her mouth. "There's a saying in Nottingham, Robin Hood has no need for a dog because he's got Little John."

Little John fired the arrow, which also went wide, and turned to shout at Marian. "Take that back! I am no dog!"

"Of course you aren't, Little John," I said, soothing the giant. "But unfortunately you missed the mark just as widely as Will Scarlet."

Little John groaned when he saw his arrow landed just above Will Scarlet's.

This, of course, made the Merry men jeer.

"Hahaha, he's in the doghouse!"

"And he was calling out Scarlet, look what happened to him!

Will Scarlet grinned wickedly. "Take your blow, Little John."

"Be a man!" Will Stutely hooted.

Much wandered off to retrieve several of the arrows off the target for me while Little John grumpily walked over to Friar Tuck.

"Sorry Little John," the Friar grinned.

"Yeah, yeah, rules are—omph," Little John grunted when Friar Tuck smashed him, sending him flying to the ground.

"I'm up," I said, flexing my wrists before I approached the firing line.

This motion raised shouts and cheers from the Merry Men as Marian handed me an arrow.

"Go, Robyn!"

"A Hood! A Hood! Robyn A Hood!"

"Good luck, Robyn!"

I carefully nocked an arrow while Much stood underneath the target, cheekily grinning at me.

"Take care not to get riled up like your best men were, Robin Hood!" Much sassily shouted.

I rolled my eyes and tossed aside my usual Robin Hood acting long enough to shout, "I have no pride, Much. You can't upset me," I said, moving the bow into the correct position.

"That man is just going to sit there?" an abbot hissed, pointing to the stationary Much.

"Robyn never misses. Not ever. He has nothing to fear," Marian carelessly shrugged.

"Hey, Robyn, your mother has the brain of a pea hen!" Much insulted, yelling from far down the archery range.

"Do not insult my mother, Much. I'll put dried apples in your clothes and let Crafty out."

"How about the King then?" Much called.

"You so much as smear his name, and I'll shoot you dead," I sneered.

"I thought you men were outlaws, bandits who worked against the king?" the head abbot asked.

"Please," Marian snorted.

"The only thing placed higher on Robyn's loyalty list than the King is God himself," Will Scarlet said, rubbing the back of his head with a wince.

"How about this? You have the bravery of a worm," Much laughed.

I sighed. "Childhood tactics aren't going to work, Much."

"Maid Marian, your fair lady, can handle a sword better than you," Much continued.

"Thank you!" Marian preened.

I rolled my eyes. "Much," I warned.

"Little John could carry you about like a toy."

"Much."

"My mother could beat you in an arm wrestling match."

"Much! I don't have any pride, but neither do I have any patience for your incessant babbling. *Silence your mouth hole!*" I shouted before moving my arrow up from the target and fixing it on the rope that held the target in the air.

I released my shot, which snapped through the rope, making the target fall directly onto Much's head.

"Ow!" he cried, plummeting to the ground.

"That will teach him," I smirked.

"Good shot, Robyn," Will Scarlet said as my Merry Men cheered for me and booed at Much.

"Yes, there's just one thing," Little John nodded.

"What?" I asked, fixing the quiver on my back.

"You missed the target," Will Scarlet reminded me.

I froze.

The humiliating hour of being dragged around by Friar Tuck replayed in my mind. "No," I whispered

"Now, now, Robyn, I've got to punish you too," the Friar sighed. Instead of cracking his knuckles and grinning deviously like he usually did before administering a punishment, he was brushing off his sleeves, clearly getting ready to lug me around again.

I wouldn't be dragged around. I couldn't!

"And I will take my punishment," I agreed after a moment of hesitation. I spun around and strode towards the visiting head abbot, who was sitting on a giant rock by the trickling river. "But I fear we have been ignoring our guests. Abbot, I ask that *you* would deal me my blow."

The abbot shifted, clearly surprised. "Are you sure? I might not be Friar Tuck, but I can administer quite a stout blow."

"I have no doubt of that," I said, cringing while remembering how I bounced off him when I ran into him that morning. He wasn't fat like Friar Tuck, but the man was a literal brick wall.

"No, Robyn," my men protested.

"You'll be hurt."

"Robyn!"

"Come now, you cannot change the rules of the game," Friar Tuck protested.

"Just this once I will," I laughed, stopping on the river bank, smiling at the abbot as he slid off his rock.

"Robyn!" the Merry Men murmured, clearly filled with concern.

"I'll take the blow for you," Little John volunteered.

"How about a re-shoot?" Will Scarlet suggested.

"Hitting the rope that strung the target in the air *might* qualify as hitting the target if we look at the technicalities," Will Stutely suggested.

"Hitting the twine, which is much smaller than the target, was more difficult!" a Merry Man shouted.

"Men!" I shouted, silencing them. "I missed the target. I'll take the blow," I said before turning back to the abbot. "Do your worst, good sir," I said as Little John and Will Scarlet pushed their way towards me.

"Are you sure?" the abbot asked again, pushing the sleeve of his robe up his arm. (His *very* muscled arm.)

I swallowed and winced. "Yes," I said, squeezing my eyes shut.

I felt the abbot shift, readying to hit me no doubt, when Will Scarlet and Little John shouted, "Robyn!"

I was abruptly pushed sideways and swayed in the air, losing my balance. I stumbled and fell right into the river.

I fell into three feet of water, soaking my entire body. I pushed myself up right and lost my hat when I rolled into deeper waters and the river bank dropped out underneath my feet.

"Little John!" I howled.

"It wasn't me, it was Will Stutely!"

"Will!" I growled, thrashing in the water before pushing my long hair out of my face. The river had already carried away my hat, so my hair tumbled down past my shoulders in a wet curtain.

"Will I'm going to *murder* you! Your mother will cry on your grave and your siblings will mourn their loss!" I promised, slapping my hands on the water when I regained my footing and started walking up the river bank.

"Every bloody time. *Every time!*" I shouted, emerging from the river. Water dripped off my clothes and clung to me like a second skin, outlining my chest. My hair hung long and loose. Even though it was soaking, it was very clearly well-kept and womanly.

A Merry Man waded knee-high into the water, holding out a blanket. I brushed him off and instead squeezed water out of my hair as more Merry Men swarmed around with concern.

"Robin Hood, the legendary outlaw… is a girl?" the head abbot asked with no small amount of disbelief.

I stepped out of the river, shaking my limbs. "Yes. Yes. Sorry for the deceit. Will, you're dead!" I bellowed before bending over to shake my head and rid my hair of more water. "I *hate* water," I uttered after popping upright.

"I can't believe it. Robin Hood, the King's champion, is a woman," the head abbot continued to muse. "How did that come about?"

I sighed and faced the monk, accepting a smaller towel from my men to wipe off my face. "It was all a misunderstanding. Some foresters were threatening Marian, I had to shoot at them. And then the Sheriff was going to have Much axed for killing a deer in Sherwood Forest. The list continues on. Everyone in my band is aware of who I really am: Robyn Smith. A girl from Nottinghamshire. It is only because of them that the legends of Robin Hood are so big. I couldn't do anything without my men."

"That's a lie!" a Merry Man shouted.

"We need Robyn more than she needs us!"

"Without her we're nothing."

"She's our master. We follow Robyn."

"Robyn is our leader—she's the only reason why the outlaws of Sherwood Forest exist. She's ours," Will Scarlet said, edging in front of me to partially hide me, Little John mimicking the movement. "We will fight for her until the day we die."

"We all love her because of her generosity, kind heart, and her love for us. It's a mutual adoration," Little John added.

"One cannot argue with such stout loyalty," the abbot said. "Very well then. I can see you are all nervous. So to assure you, I shall share a secret of my own," the head abbot said before pushing back the hood of his robe.

His face was strong and sure. He had chiseled features, a solid mouth, a blonde beard, stormy blue eyes, and noble blonde hair. It was a face I had seen daily for the past eleven days. It was the face of the King.

"King Richard," I whispered before collapsing to my knees.

One by one, the Merry Men mirrored my movement.

"I have been told so much about you, Robyn Hood. You robbed my brother and stole from my lords in order to raise funds for my ransom," King Richard said as the rest of the abbots slowly pushed off the hoods of their cowls. They were the lords who traveled with the King; I recognized every last one of them from the daily processions.

"I heard of the time you stormed Nottingham to save Little John and Will Scarlet," King Richard continued. "How you protected the beautiful Maid Marian from the greedy Sir Guy of Gisborne, how you won the famed archery contest, earning that very arrow that hangs over your camp. I have heard so many ballads and tales about you, Robyn Hood."

"I am sorry, Sire, that I cannot live up to them," I whispered, hanging my head.

"No, you surpassed your ballads, Robyn," the King laughed.

"Sire?" I asked, my eyes shooting up to meet his gaze.

"Your Merry Men are not merely loyal—they adore you. The

people of Nottinghamshire would rather die than tell the Sheriff where you are. You inspire love and adoration wherever you go. I would love to have such a person serve me," King Richard benevolently smiled.

"My King?" I breathed.

"Robyn Hood, I officially pardon you and all of your Merry Men. Will you join my courts and serve me for the rest of your days?" the King asked.

I blinked back the tears and smiled before bending over again to look at the ground. "I will."

"Then rise, Robyn Hood," King Richard ordered.

I slowly stood even though the rest of my men continued to kneel. I briefly twisted around to glance at my men, my eyes resting on Will Scarlet. I owed him more than a mere pardon. I owed *all* my men more than a pardon. "Sire, if I have won any of your affection, may I make a request?"

"Hm?" the King asked as his lords twittered behind him.

"Please, sire. Return Will Scarlet's title to him. He is William Gamwell, rightful Earl of Maxfield. He was outlawed for killing a man who was trying to assassinate him. Please grant Marian a pardon too. Her parents are terribly angry with her for associating with me. And as you have probably figured out, the love between Robin Hood and Maid Marian is a sham forged to protect me," I hesitated before gazing out at my band. "Every last one of them has special circumstances. I can't just toss them back, my lord. Even if you pardon them."

King Richard laughed. "You really are the king of this forest. Very well, Robyn Hood. I shall see to it that every last one of your Merry Men will be well cared for. Any that would care to enter my services are welcome to. Any that would prefer to return home can do so with an easy mind."

"Thank you, sire," I bowed.

The cheers from the Merry Men were thunderous.

We had a wonderful afternoon. After I changed out of my soggy clothes and reclaimed my hat from Crafty's teeth (the black horse had gotten out of his pen and was splashing in the river when my hat floated past him), the men and I dueled and fought with cudgels.

King Richard proved to be an even match for Will Scarlet, our best swordsman, and one of the lords nearly beat Little John at the staff.

When we heard horns trumpeting at the edge of Sherwood, and two scouts returned from patrol to inform me a procession was waiting for King Richard, my band of Merry Men and I escorted the monarch to his waiting parade.

"I will publicly pardon you when I return to London and my courts. However, I am not sure when I will see you again, for I plan to leave the shores of Britain in a week or so," the King said as we walked.

"You're leaving so soon?" I asked.

"Phillip, the French King, is eyeing my Angevin Empire. I will die before I see him have it," King Richard vowed.

My Merry Men and I winced.

"Do not worry, even if I am not present, my courts will treat you kindly. My mother is a deep admirer of yours," King Richard chuckled.

"About that, Your Majesty. I really have no desire to work in a court. I am an ignorant peasant. Even with my pardon, I am not eager to reveal Robin Hood's true gender," I hesitantly supplied.

"It matters not. You are a capable woman, Robyn," King Richard insisted.

"My King," Marian said with a devious grin. "You have Will Scarlet to his rightful position. I would bet my father's castle on Robyn becoming a countess and joining your courts in a matter of months."

"Marian!" I hissed, turning red.

King Richard laughed. "So be it. I look forward to receiving tidings of your wedding, Lord William."

I crankily pulled my hat lower on my head, meticulously checking to make sure no long locks were peeking out of the cap.

Three steps later, and we were in front of King Richard's procession.

"Thank you for honoring us with your presence, My King," I said, bowing. The rest of the Merry Men kneeled and murmured similar thank-yous.

"The pleasure was mine, Robyn Hood," the King smiled, nodding at the servant who brought forth a beautiful white horse. "I am glad I met you. And I am equally relieved to hear that the stone in my horse's hoof was from you," he wryly added.

I blushed darker and muttered at the ground.

King Richard laughed again. "I will send word from London after your pardon is public. My brother won't be able to touch you. Thank you, Robin Hood, and Merry Men, for your service. Please, rise," he ordered.

We all got to our feet and beamed at our monarch.

"Farewell, take care," King Richard wished.

"You as well, Sire. May God protect you," I said.

"Thank you," King Richard said. He started to mount up his horse but paused and backed away. "I can't help it," he announced before reaching out and grabbing me.

I was shocked witless when he aimed his face down and kissed me.

And it wasn't a short kiss.

Oh no.

I can't say I remember much of it, mostly because I had the overwhelming feeling of shock flooding through my body. I do remember his blonde beard tickled my face.

When he let me go, I stared at him and stumbled backwards, only to be steadied by Marian.

"*King Richard!*" several of the lords-disguised-as-abbots shouted.

"What will people *say!*" they cried, clearly indicating that the rest of the procession didn't know I was a girl.

Indeed the gossip had already started up.

"Did you know our King was like *that?*" one boy who held a trumpet muttered to a boy holding a flag.

"No. But clearly he is," the flag boy replied.

"King Richard!" Will Scarlet and Little John also shouted, although for a very different reason than his lords.

"You just—you just!" Will Scarlet sputtered.

"Took advantage of our leader!" Little John thumped.

King Richard laughed as he swung onto the back of his horse. "What… jealous you didn't get to Robyn first?"

"*King Richard!*" his lords screamed.

King Richard turned his horse and rode away, raising a hand in farewell. His lords and procession hurried after him, gossiping and muttering the whole way.

"—ruined his hard-earned reputation in a single day thanks to some pretty face."

My Merry Men and I watched them go in shocked silence.

"Well. That was interesting," Marian chirped.

"Did that really happen, or did I imagine it all?" I asked in a dazed voice.

"That *King,*" Will Scarlet hissed, angrily eyeing the dazzling procession.

"He's lucky he's leaving Britain," Little John chuckled before gesturing for us all to return to the forest.

Will Scarlet was still scowling as we plunged back into the foliage.

"Is something wrong?" I asked, slowing down.

Will Scarlet nailed me with a rather accusing look, and I blushed bright red. I was about to make tracks and escape Scarlet's bad temper when Little John unfortunately foresaw my plan and waylaid it by sweeping out a tree trunk arm. He caught me in the chest and heaved me backwards, throwing me to the ground.

"Oh, sorry, Robyn. I didn't see you there," he said, sounding not at all apologetic as I coughed and hacked, trying to get air to my lungs. Perhaps he was still a little sore that I chose Will.

I heard a Merry Man, Much probably, murmuring further down the path. Little John replied in his deep tones, "She is fine. Will Scarlet can wait with her. We had best return to camp and clean up."

Little John stomped away like a giant as I hesitantly propped myself up on my elbows. Marian and the Merry Men went with him, occasionally glancing back over their shoulders to look at me.

I tried to beg for someone else to stay, but I couldn't speak with the air still knocked out of me and breathed like a wheezing dog. I breathed deeply in the new silence of the forest and glanced fretfully to Will Scarlet—who was crouched next to me with a thoughtful look.

"Are you really that terrified of me?" he asked. Although his voice was friendly, I could tell it pained him to ask.

"No," I said after taking several gulps of air.

"Then why are you so frightened of facing me when it comes to love? I have been patient, and I haven't pushed you much. You must be either scared stiff of me, or you don't love me at all and you're avoiding me," Will Scarlet said, standing up. "Which one is it, Robyn?"

I shook my head. "Neither," I said as I stumbled to my feet.

"Then what is it that makes you so unwilling?"

I stared at my feet and did not answer.

Will sighed before walking away from me. "I see. I will take care to not be caught alone with you again. I wouldn't want to further impede you."

"Will!" I shouted, hurrying after him. "Wait, it's none of that."

"Oh?"

"I, I just don't know if this is real," I lamely said.

Will Scarlet stopped, staring straight ahead. "You doubt that I really *love* you? Do you think me to be that fickle?" he asked, finally turning to look at me.

"Yes. No. What I mean is you're a Lord's son! Even if you *love* me there's no possible way you can *marry* me," I explained.

A shadow of a smile finally found its way to Will Scarlet's lips. "Robyn, you have robbed a prince and saved a King, and you speak of impossibilities?"

"Aren't you like Marian? Do you not have to marry another member of nobility?" I said.

"That's what this is about?" Will Scarlet said, his eyebrows rising. "Oh Robyn, you should have said something sooner," he said before taking a step closer to me and folding his arms around me.

Although I was tense and closely imitated a plank of wood, Will Scarlet was warm and gentle as he rested his chin on the top of my head. "I'm aware that you just went and got my title back for me, but it's not important to me. Robyn, when I joined your band, I gave up everything—my claim to my title, my family— because I believed in you and what you were doing. My feelings have only increased since then. I would gladly stay with you in Sherwood *forever* if that is what you wished. If you are afraid that I will not marry you because of a silly title, then I do not want it. My younger brother can have it, I care not. *You* are what I desire, Robyn. You are what my waking moments are about. I will follow you until I am physically unable to, and I will love you until the last beat of my heart."

I was quiet as I leaned into Will Scarlet, finding comfort in his declaration.

He was quiet for a few moments until he gently stepped back, placing his fingers under my chin to tip my head upright. "So Robyn, my heart's desire, do you accept my love? Do you return it?"

I thoughtfully studied Will's face. He had to become a lord. He needed to. Will Scarlet was the *one* member of my band that would hold a reasonable amount of power now that we were pardoned. At the same time, though, I did love him. I loved him for what he did, for his valiance and gentleness, for his kindness, concern, and love. I loved Will Scarlet. What frightened me was that I loved him so much I was willing to become a lady to stay with him. The idea of being a noble was even more terrifying than Marian's Outlaw Dream ever was.

I nodded, unable to speak at first. "I do, Will."

Will Scarlet smiled as if I had just saved his life and given him his greatest wish in the span of one moment. His smile turned mischievous as he leaned in, touching his forehead against mine. "So you'll take on my last name as my *wife*, **not** my cousin?"

I winced. "I was wondering if you picked up on that."

"I did. I just about slugged that George fellow when he took you from me at the party. The fact that he called you Lady Gamwell is the only thing that saved him."

"How big of you," I laughed when Scarlet's breath tickled my face.

"Indeed. And King Richard… I cannot say I'm sorry to see him go."

"*Will*! He's our King!"

"Yes and he kissed you first even though you're going to be *my* wife. That is a rather high, not to mention unfair, tax," Will Scarlet, his lips grazing my cheek.

"It's one kiss, Will. What is a kiss compared to a lifetime?" I sighed.

Will pulled back for a moment and blinked at me before softly smiling. "Yes, a lifetime," he agreed before leaning in and kissing me.

At first I tried to squirm away, but Will would not let me go. He kept kissing me until I leaned into him, the strength of my legs abandoning me against the romantic onslaught.

His kiss was *vastly* different from King Richard's. It was longer, yes, but unlike the King, Will would not allow me to be shocked. It was passionate, consuming, and it oddly felt as though my heart were a target, and Will had just hit the dead center with a well-placed arrow.

It also made me senselessly stupid.

Will finally pulled back and I slumped against his shoulder, unable to form coherent words.

"Maybe it's just as well it took so long to kiss you," Will said, his voice rough. "The wait for our wedding would have killed me."

"Pfehwd," I said into his neck.

"I agree," Will said, hugging me closer before leaning down.

Before he could kiss me again, Much burst out of the underbrush. "Alright, that's enough. No more kissing! You have to stay a horse length away from her until you're officially married. I said no more kissing—Will Stutely, seize Robyn!" he shouted.

I almost fell over in surprise, but Will Scarlet was holding most of my weight already.

Will Stutely circled us, clucking and lecturing me about kisses and spiritual ruin as more Merry Men joined us.

Will Scarlet laughed and swung me through the air before he set off, carrying me through the forest. "Be useful for once and summon the good Friar Tuck, Much. Tell him he has a wedding to preside over!"

WHEN KING RICHARD left for the Angevin Empire, he never again set foot on Britannica's shores alive. He died five years after I met him, in a siege on the castle of Chalus.

After that, Prince John was crowned King John.

He was, as predicted, a tyrant who laid a severe taxation on Britain. He had inherited difficulties to be sure—King Richard's ongoing feud with France was a heavy burden—but he treated his own followers with ingratitude and was generally lazy and slothful. He angered the Catholic Church because of his marriages and divorce as well as the whole Archbishop of Canterbury episode. Not to mention that he alienated the lower British class with his taxes and forest laws.

That alienation gave his barons the chance they needed to weaken the British crown forever. And as the people's (secret) champion, I had to help them.

10

ONE LAST RIDE

I leaned forward and squinted through the trees as my horse, Conniving, thundered along. "We're catching up," I shouted to Rodger. Rodger of Wendover, a monk and chronicler.

"'We're catching up,' she said. I'll have to write that down," Rodger shouted back, gripping his leggy chestnut horse while eyeing the saddlebag thrown over the front of his saddle. That saddlebag held his inks and papers.

Yes. Rodger of Wendover. A monk and chronicler, and a major thorn in my side. Whose brilliant idea was it for me to drag a scholar with me while trying to change the course of the future?

"I told you already, you can't write about *any* of this for that blasted *Historic Flowers* book!" I shouted back.

"I'm going to call it *Flores Historiarum*, Flowers of History! And I haven't started it…yet," Rodger shouted, offended.

I rolled my eyes and adjusted my position before Conniving jumped a fallen tree that was in our path. "Why are you with me again?"

"Because Alan-A-Dale and I flipped a coin to see who could

watch you root out King John and write about it. He lost," Rodger said.

"That's right, Marian would only lend you one swift horse," I muttered into Conniving's black mane. The black horse snorted, as though answering me.

Conniving was a fast horse. He wasn't as stocky as my previous horses, Crafty, Cunning, and Cranky, but he was as swift as they came.

As Conniving jumped another tree, a part of my heart twanged in pain. Years ago, I had spent afternoons with Crafty like this, racing through Sherwood Forest at top speed. But so much had changed since then.

First of all, Crafty was dead and buried years ago. Secondly, as I'm sure you have predicted, I was now Countess Robyn Gamwell, the mother of three and wife of William Gamwell, Earl of Maxfield.

Since King Richard's death sixteen years prior, I had regrouped my Merry Men. Only now we weren't outlaws in a forest. We were lords in King John's court. We were stewards in the highest castles. We were ranking officers in the army. We wouldn't often rob in Sherwood Forest anymore, but we were a bigger threat to King John now more than ever.

It was the year 1215, and I was out to kill King John's power.

I meant to seize him and hold him until his barons pranced in and forced him to sign a document called "Articles of the Barons." The articles themselves were important, but the most significant part of them was clause 61. Clause 61 would establish a committee of 25 barons who could, at any time, overrule whatever King John proclaimed. They could even seize his possessions and castles if they liked.

William, known as Will Scarlet, my husband, had explained the importance of this clause to me time and time again as I threw together a few possessions and set out to hunt down King John so he would sign it.

(The dratted monarch had fled at the first sound of forcing him to sign it.)

"Make him seal it, Robyn," Will had said, gripping my hand before kissing it, his eyes dark with love in spite of the urgency at the moment. "It will give England a fighting chance again. He's going to *ruin* us."

I snapped out of my memories when Conniving nearly rammed me into a tree branch.

"He wanted to come with, you know," Rodger called to me, wincing as he bounced on the chestnut's back.

"Who?" I called.

"William. Your husband," Rodger replied.

I nodded and felt behind me to make sure my longbow was still properly secured. Riding without Will was like riding with a missing limb. His absence was a gaping hole in my heart. "He didn't have much of a choice. He's already under close analysis for being a member of Robin Hood's band of Merry Men. And someone needed to stay behind and keep things in order," I said, more to remind myself than to explain the situation to Rodger.

"He wasn't happy your other men got to come," Rodger laughed.

"Much got permission from his wife, and his eldest is old enough to run the mill by himself. Gilbert is on leave from the army, and Little John's wife practically kicked him off their small manor. I believe she said he would be sleeping with the pigs unless he got King John to sign those papers," I laughed, feeling a little better. I was very fond of Little John's wife, Lady Isabella. She was fiery, brash, and as sweet as a newborn filly.

Conniving snorted, white foam dripping from his mouth. Both he and Rodger's horse were sweaty. The only thing that kept me from worrying that we might not catch King John was that I knew the horse he had taken from the Royal Stables didn't have the stamina necessary to outrun my Conniving.

"Keep it up boy," I murmured to my mount.

I grinned when I saw a flash of red dart through the trees ahead.

"This is it. We've got him, Rodger," I shouted before unhooking my longbow. My rabbit skin quiver, which was filled with arrows fletched with my familiar grey, speckled feathers, was already in place on my back.

Seconds later, Rodger and I burst into a meadow. That's when I caught full sight of him: King John.

He was in front of us, only a stone's throw away, riding his horse hard. The animal was slick with sweat and was fairing worse than Conniving or Rodger's chestnut.

King John was just as bad as his horse. He wore a red cape, and for once he had the good sense not to nestle his crown on his head. However, his hair was plastered to his head, and he kept twisting around. No doubt he had heard Conniving's thunderous hooves.

"Halt, King John!" I shouted, nocking an arrow.

Over the years, my archery ability had not weakened in the least, thanks to continual practice. (Being the wife of a pardoned outlaw, even if he was still nobility, gave me a lot of leeway in choosing my hobbies.)

The King squealed and kicked his horse.

I released the first arrow, which shot clean through his red cape.

"Good aim!" Rodger complimented, still jostling on his horse's back.

King John did not stop, although he did emit a rather high-pitched scream.

I released another shot. This time the arrow grazed so closely to his head I'm sure I cut off a lock of his hair.

Still King John pressed forward.

I grumbled before shouting to Rodger, "Look out! I'm going to catch him," I said before unclasping the few saddlebags I had packed. I pushed them off Conniving's rump, getting rid of the excess weight.

"Come on, boy. *Run!*" I sang to my horse.

He responded beautifully.

Conniving stretched out and picked up speed as we galloped through the meadow.

When we pulled aside the King's horse, Conniving slammed into the animal, and I pushed King John straight off the side.

King John toppled to the ground as I turned Conniving around and pulled him into a prancing trot.

King John rolled to his feet and started running for the edge of the forest. In a second, I had an arrow nocked and aimed. I released it, and it caught the corner of his cape, pinning it to the ground.

King John abandoned the cape, ripping it off his shoulders, and continued to run away, even when I pulled Conniving into a tight circle around him. He victoriously leaped at the tree line, but was forced to halt in his tracks when I nailed him to a tree with a well-placed arrow that dug through his clothes.

"No!" King John moaned. "Let me go! I'll give you anything!"

Conniving blew hard and tossed his head as I uneasily kept another arrow trained on the sweating King John.

"Well done, Robyn!" Rodger praised from his horse's back as the animal walked forward, stopping a short distance away. "And so King John was cornered in Runnymede Meadow," he said, digging in his saddlebag, pulling out a piece of paper.

I slid off Conniving and slowly ambled up to King John, an arrow still nocked in my bowstring. "King John, you are going to sign the Articles of the Barons," I told him, exhaling deeply. (I was starting to be too old for this.)

"I assure you, Madame, if you release me I will reward you for —" He froze then squinted when he saw my face. "You are Countess Gamwell, wife to that infuriating Earl of Maxfield. Of course *you* would be the one to capture me," he grumbled. "Your blasted husband has no spine against you—"

"Curb your tongue, King John," I warned, poking him in the nose with the sharp tip of my arrow. "Lest I become tempted to rid Britain of you forever."

"I'll have you killed for your insolence!" King John promised.

I couldn't help it. I laughed. "How many times have you said that in the past, and it's *never* come true. Give it up, King John," I laughed.

"What?" King John muttered as sweat trickled down the side of his face. He was growing nervous and was too frazzled to notice my implication. "Y-you can't hurt me," he continued. "Release me, you barbaric woman!"

"Rodger, you have a crossbow?"

"Yes," Rodger said, almost falling off his horse.

"Load it and keep it trained on King John," I ordered.

Rodger unhooked the crossbow and did as I asked. "I don't understand. What are you—oh! Is this the famed call I've heard so much about?" he excitedly said.

"Keep your eye on the King, Rodger," I warned as I felt through my skirts before finding what I was looking for, my white horn.

King John turned ghost white. "No," he whispered.

I brought the horn to my lips and blew three quick blasts.

"It can't be," King John shook.

"But it is," Rodger assured the shaken man.

"Rodger, shut your mouth," I warned.

King John was staring at my face with horror. "Robin Hood," he uttered. "He gave that to you didn't he? I knew he wasn't dead! He couldn't be dead! Every few years, another ballad about him would pop out of the woodwork. I'll have his head when I'm finished with you!" he snarled.

King John was right, to a degree. I hadn't completely given up Robin Hood yet. Occasionally, Little John and my closest men and I would return to Sherwood to rob for a fortnight or two and make more memories. Alan-A-Dale was usually with us, hence the ballads.

"Where is he?" King John continued. "He's behind this whole mess, isn't he?"

"King John, I would be more worried about your barons than Robin Hood at this moment," I smirked.

"Are you sure I can't write about this?" Rodger complained. "History should reflect the truth!"

"Not all truths. Leave Robin Hood and his Merry Men out of your history compilation, Rodger. We make the water murky enough already," I said, my eyes tracing the edges of the meadow. "There they are," I said as two horses exited the forest and galloped in my direction.

I waved my hand to greet my second-in-command and first Merry Man: Little John and Much the miller.

"I told you we needed to catch him. Those barons of his are *slow*," I said to my men as they pounded up to us, pulling their horses into skidding halts just short of Conniving.

"I didn't argue that his barons were slow, I simply thought it might be too dangerous," Much argued, dismounting with Little John.

"I knew you could catch him," Little John said.

"Where's Gilbert?" I asked as my men left their horses and wandered to my side.

"Guiding the barons here. They should arrive in several minutes."

"Perfect. Rodger, enjoy chronicling your history. I shall see you again sometime in the future," I said before motioning at Much. "Keep your weapons trained on the King, Much. He's anxious to get away from his barons."

"Are you sure you won't stay?" Rodger asked.

"The barons wouldn't be suspicious of Robin Hood's men aiding them, but they might find it odd that it was Countess

Gamwell who caught their miscreant King. I cannot afford to bring myself under further scrutiny, Rodger. I have to go," I said. "Much, please stay behind with Rodger to guard King John. I'll meet you back in London later tonight," I said, fixing my horn back into the folds of my skirts. (Traipsing around the countryside in a dress was *not* entertaining. I still have no idea how Marian managed it for so long when we were stationed in Sherwood.)

I started towards Conniving, Little John behind me.

"Tell him I'll find him, and I'll kill him!" King John vowed.

I paused and turned around. "What?"

"Tell Robin Hood that I am coming for him! He can't hide from me forever! I shall *ruin* him for this!" King John hissed.

I narrowed my eyes and stalked back towards the monarch. I couldn't stand it anymore. Someone had to set the lazy, overgrown brat straight.

"Listen to me," I growled, reaching out to grab King John by the throat.

He cried out but settled down when I squeezed his neck.

"Listen long and hard, King John. Robin Hood is not afraid of you. He's never gone into hiding, he never ran away from you, he's been dogging your every step," I whispered in his ear. "Robin Hood has never let you out of his sight, King John. And I never will," I said before pushing him back against the tree.

King John looked shocked and confused before glancing at the arrow that held him pinned to the tree. As he stared at the grey, speckled fletching, Robin Hood's trademark, he finally realized. "*You*," he said, his mouth a-gap. "You are Robin Hood!"

I smirked before cruelly laughing. "I am. And I have danced in your courts and eaten in your halls. Be afraid, King John. I can follow you wherever you go. And if you endanger this country any further... I will take care of you," I uttered before twisting around and stalking away.

I fastened my longbow over Conniving's back, along with the saddlebags Little John had kindly retrieved.

After securing everything, Little John helped me struggle onto Conniving. (Mounting and sitting astride in skirts is a clumsy practice.)

"Remember, King John," I cheerfully called as Little John mounted his horse. I could see flags and horses moving at the far end of the meadow. "I could have killed you all of those years ago when I robbed your carriage. Sign the articles, my King. Or there's no telling where I'll pop up next time," I said before urging Conniving into a slow canter.

Little John and I rode out of Runnymede meadow, disappearing from sight just as King John's barons piled in.

"We should make it home in less than a day. I hope Isabella will make her cinnamon bread for me. Ah, that was well done, Robyn," Little John praised as we pulled our horses into a companionable walk.

"Thank you," I smiled.

"You should be thankful. Since Alan isn't here he won't dare make another ballad," he teased.

"I've had enough ballads to last me a lifetime," I groaned.

"But they're so catchy," Little John argued before launching into one, his baritone voice echoing through the forest.

> *"Robin Hood he was and a tall young man,*
> *Derry derry down*
> *And fifteen winters old,*
> *And Robin Hood he was a proper young man,*
> *Of courage stout and bold.*
> *Hey down derry derry down."*

"I really must set Alan on making a Robin Hood death ballad. I'm getting to be too old for this, and I tire of leaving my family for outlaw business. I have a cousin, the prioress of Kirkly. She offered to be the villain of the story and kill me."

"Aye, I can understand that. I miss Isabella fiercely when we ride. But, I beg your pardon, who on earth would *want* to be responsible for 'killing' Robin Hood?" Little John asked.

"She's sort of a nut," I admitted.

"That explains it," Little John laughed before singing a different ballad.

> "When Robin Hood was about twenty years old,
> With a hey down down and a down
> He happened to meet Little John,
> A jolly brisk blade, right fit for the trade,
> For he was a lusty young man."

"If you're going to sing the whole way back to London, I'll leave you behind," I threatened.

"Ahhh, such companionship," Little John hummed.

"If Will hears you insinuate anything about that again, he'll demote you," I warned.

"I'm more afraid of Marian than I am of him," Little John said, continuing to hum.

"I would be more afraid of your wife," I countered.

"Oh yes, *I* would be. But she just runs my knightly life; Maid Marian, on the other hand, has gone off and married a duke—the poor man. There's a great chance her husband will be one of the barons running the country with King John's powers being practically neutered and all."

"Now that's a scary thought," I shuddered. Indeed, Marian's husband *did* dote on her. (He kept a variable stable of horses to be used for her pleasure alone.) If she asked him to do something…

In my pondering silence, Little John sang another ballad.

'But he shall be a bold yeoman of mine,
My chief man next to thee;
And I Robin Hood, and thou Little John,
And Scarlet he shall be.'

'And we'll be three of the bravest outlaws
That is in the North Country.'
If you will have any more of bold Robin Hood,
In his second part it will be.'

"Hold your tongue or I'll cut it off," I crossly said.

"Nay! Robyn Hood would never commit such an act! It says so in the ballads."

"A plague on you, Alan-A-Dale! I hate your stupid ballads!"

The End

OTHER SERIES BY K. M. SHEA

The Snow Queen

Timeless Fairy Tales

The Fairy Tale Enchantress

The Elves of Lessa

Hall of Blood and Mercy

Court of Midnight and Deception

Pack of Dawn and Destiny

King Arthur and Her Knights

Robyn Hood

The Magical Beings' Rehabilitation Center

Second Age of Retha: Written under pen name A. M. Sohma

ADDITIONAL NOVELS

Life Reader

Princess Ahira

A Goose Girl

ABOUT THE AUTHOR

K. M. Shea is a fantasy-romance author who never quite grew out of adventure books or fairy tales, and still searches closets in hopes of stumbling into Narnia. She is addicted to sweet romances, witty characters, and happy endings. She also writes LitRPG and GameLit under the pen name, A. M. Sohma.

Printed in Great Britain
by Amazon